"I DON'T OWE YOU A THING!" SHE SCREAMED.

"You accosted me on my own property and disappeared, and now—"

"Accosted?" he asked mockingly.

"All right. Seduced!" Serena snapped.

"Objection! I'm sure you're the one who seduced me," he contradicted quietly.

"The hell I did! I was going swimming—"

"Do you often do things like that?"

"Of course not," she answered, confused.

"What was it then, Mrs. Loren—magic?"

Serena paused and then began again. "Dr. O'Neill, don't you see how pointless this all is?"

"No, I don't, because you can't ignore what happened between us. And, Serena"—he bent toward her, holding her face in his hands—"I won't let you."

A CANDLELIGHT ECSTASY ROMANCE®

SERENA'S MAGIC

Heather Graham

A CANDLELIGHT ECSTASY ROMANCE®

Published by
Dell Publishing Co., Inc.
1 Dag Hammarskjold Plaza
New York, New York 10017

ISBN: 0-440-17860-6

Printed in the United States of America

First printing—September 1984

For Mary Torres

To Our Readers:

We have been delighted with your enthusiastic response to Candlelight Ecstasy Romances®, and we thank you for the interest you have shown in this exciting series.

In the upcoming months we will continue to present the distinctive, sensuous love stories you have come to expect only from Ecstasy. We look forward to bringing you many more books from your favorite authors and also the very finest work from new authors of contemporary romantic fiction.

As always, we are striving to present the unique, absorbing love stories that you enjoy most—books that are more than ordinary romance.

Your suggestions and comments are always welcome. Please write to us at the address below.

Sincerely,

The Editors
Candlelight Romances
1 Dag Hammarskjold Plaza
New York, New York 10017

PROLOGUE

It was dusk. Spectral vision time. And surely she was a vision, an illusion of dusk, of dreams. As he opened his eyes, she was simply there, across the expanse of the clear water now growing dark as the sun lowered from the sky to hover on the horizon before dipping beneath it. The day was bathed in that yellow and orange haze that came just for a short, magical time before darkness. An hour ago it had been hot, but now, here, with the dampness of the water rising and the sun setting, there was a slight chill, adding to the feeling of misted illusion. Where the water would still be warm from the day, the air was already becoming damp and cool with the coming of night.

And suddenly, as if part of the mystical illusion, she appeared.

Against the chill, she wore a cloak. A black cloak.

For a moment she merely gazed into the water, then her head lifted and her eyes calmly scanned the pond and her side of the shoreline. Then she spun about, a wealth of chestnut hair floating around her like a gold-tinged mantle. And as she circled, she raised her arms, and the black cape fell open. He saw that beneath it she was beautifully and splendidly . . . naked.

She stood there—for what must only have been seconds, but as he stared with shock and disbelief, it seemed like an eternity.

An eternity in which he revered and memorized every subtlety of her ivory flesh. In those few seconds he noted that her eyes were dark and stunningly deep and luminous; her nose was slender but long, although slightly tilted and arrogant; her face was part oval, part heart; her lips, in the distant light of dusk, were incredibly shaped, full and sensuously curving, as if she held all the secrets of the pool, and of the realm of twilight and dusk.

She appeared tall with the black cloak floating behind her. She was neither slim nor heavy, but some plane of perfection in between. Her high, full breasts were tipped with deep rouge, proud and inviting. They lusciously curved above a long, slender ribcage that tapered neatly to a minuscule waistline, the ivory skin like satin as it dipped in twilight shadow to the hollow of her belly. Her enticing hips were invitingly curved and angled to her long and shapely legs. They were slim and wickedly lithe, but strong and firm. It would occur to him later that he even noticed her feet; they too were long, and slender, just like her hands with the elegant fingers that stretched out in that embrace to the harbor of the trees.

Totally unaware of him, she was at ease with her surroundings. It was as if she were a part of the soft breeze, and of the foliage and the earth. There was something so sensual and provocative about her very innocence that he was staggered by a shaft of the most shattering raw desire he had ever experienced. Yet even that desire was touched by magic; it was a very male need to conquer and to dominate with selfish possession, but it was tempered by a tender need to cherish.

She stretched high, the gleaming ivory of her body glistening in the soft light, then the cloak fell about her feet and she disappeared into the water, making its crystal surface ripple in tiny waves.

He realized then that every muscle in his body had tensed, that a sheen of perspiration lay over his skin. His breathing suddenly sounded terribly harsh and shallow in the quiet of the clearing. The desire that had surged like a storm tempest within him at first sight of this spectacle surged through him with a full, pulsing, thundering sensation, filling his ears with the hammer of need. He wanted to laugh at himself, but he couldn't. The sound caught in his throat. He had to harshly remind himself that she was not a dream or a vision, but a real woman, believing herself alone, appreciating her little heaven and her privacy.

He was an intruder. One only attacked wood nymphs in dreams, and he wasn't dreaming. Or was he? No. She had disappeared, but the black cloak that had shielded her lay upon the earth in evidence that she did exist.

He should leave. Silently disappear and leave her to her innocent solitude. But though the ages had bred a man civil enough not to simply attack, there was enough primitivism left in the male so that he could neither be perfect gentleman enough to simply leave when he was spellbound by this strange magic. . . .

He had never played the pickup games at bars; he had never made up ridiculous lines. But now he was in a quandary. He wanted to meet her, but it would be rather absurd to walk up and introduce himself to a naked woman. Not a woman, he thought with a strange touch of whimsy, a witch. A beautiful witch. This was, after all, Salem.

Her head popped up in the water. She stood, waist high, and smoothed back her dripping hair. Again she plunged beneath the surface.

The pond wasn't more than a hundred yards wide. Impulsively he stood, realizing he must have slept long, as his previously soaked cutoffs had dried. Plans were spinning in his mind as he entered the water and dove deep.

In spite of the cooling of the surrounding twilight air, the water seemed warm, retaining that touch of the sun. He surfaced for air, then plunged again. This time he found her. Those long legs moved gracefully against the crystal of the water. Her well-molded form was inviting, enticing him to touch.

She folded to plunge into another dive, her body naturally agile in the liquid playground. But as she dove down, her outstretched hand touched him and her eyes opened wide with horror.

Of all things, he hadn't meant to send her into a panic. He shot to the surface after her, just in time to hear her scream echo in a gasp through the shelter of the trees. She hadn't had much time to fill her lungs with air, and therefore her scream was more gasp than clamorous sound.

"Hey," he muttered quickly, "I'm sorry, I thought I was alone." His lie was bold—and astonishingly convincing. He grinned to try to ease the terror in her eyes, but she hadn't had a chance to recover enough from her shock to catch her breath, and treading water, she slipped back beneath the surface to arise again choking and sputtering. Concern then outweighed everything. He slipped an arm beneath her breast and began to tow her into shore, heedless of whether she protested his touch or not.

But still he noticed that her flesh had the feel of the silk he thought it; she was warm; the vibrancy of life pulsed through her; the full curve of her breasts was as firm and sensual as distance had hinted.

He reached the shoreline, assured himself that she was breathing, and procured her cloak and slipped it around her shoulders. She accepted it, fingers clutching the material close to her throat. He realized then that her eyes were so dark a blue as to be truly violet. Her hands and fingers were as delicately elegant as her feet, the nails medium length, and touched by that same coral bronze.

"I'm sorry," he murmured again. Those beautiful, deep eyes were upon him, reflecting the liquid mystery of the pond. He couldn't know then that she was staring quite as he had. In a bit of shock she was thinking he was the most perfect male she had ever seen. He might have walked out of a page of ancient history; he was as broad-shouldered and fully, sleekly muscled as a gladiator in a Roman arena; or perhaps he was more like a barbarian who had roamed the lands of prehistory, surviving by wit and agility and whatever raw strength and courage he could create. Water from the pond dripped in rivulets from his physique, glistening on the bronze of his flesh, enunciating the strong delineations of his finely toned chest. Even his abdomen, tight and trim, rippled with clean, wire-fine sinews.

It was his face she actually stared at; strange how her vision had first taken in his body. But then, it was an extraordinary body.

She drew her attention to the face of the man. Her first thought was that it was a strong face. The chin was clean-shaven and firm, the mouth full but taut, touched at the corners by faint lines that hinted of both an ability to smile and an ability to harden relentlessly. His nose was straight, proudly prominent, reminding her a bit of a great bird of flight, an eagle or a hawk.

His eyes were piercing crystals, a deep hazel which she quickly saw could burn with a brown so dark as to be night or lighten with a green that could be springtime and sunshine. In seconds she read many things in those eyes, while also knowing that the depths of the man were such that he would be difficult to ever know. Yet there was some type of instant recognition. She sensed that he could burn with the intensity of raging fire, laugh with the freedom of the air, and love with wild, tempestuous abandon, recklessly demanding and giving beyond the bounds of earth.

How ridiculous, she thought. I do not know this man; he has suddenly appeared, and this is really an absurd situation. I'm sitting here more naked than clothed with a total stranger.

"You're trespassing," she said, intending to sound indignant as she drew her cloak even more tightly against her.

He loved the indigo snap of her eyes with the righteous anger. "I'm sorry—I didn't realize this was private property." He made no effort to move, but remained stooped beside her. There was a scent to him, she thought, that was not cologne. It was a faint, but pleasant manly scent, and something more. It was stirring, and it touched her blood as did his probing, intense stare. She wanted to say more; she wanted to escape because absurdly she was beginning to feel that she was sinking, and that if she didn't quickly find an edge to grasp, she would be

15

forever lost. She parted her lips slightly, but no sound came from her because he was speaking, and his voice was deep and husky, and ungodly rich.

"I never believed," he said, "that eyes could be truly violet. But yours are. . . ."

It wasn't a line; he spoke with true incredulity. And as he moved closer to her, it wasn't by conscious effort. It was something older even than time, more elusive than magic. That same elemental recognition, perhaps. But his lips touched hers, and it was lightning, a burst of starfire, dawn and moonlit midnight all in one. She should repel him she thought; she should move away with furious condemnation.

She arched her throat to better feel the sensations of his lips and taste the sweet salt of his mouth. Her tongue touched his, and as they deeply explored each other's mouths, his arms came around her, and they were as strong and secure as the glistening muscles hinted. He bore her back against the earth at the water's edge, and she moved with him without protest, lost to all normal reasoning. She was ruled by an emotion more intense than any she had ever experienced, and the single thought that permeated that emotion was that in her heart she knew this man . . . she had always been waiting for him. She had been born for this moment, for this man who had appeared like an apparition from the crystal of the pond. Being held by him, touched by him, was as natural as the breeze, as the high grasses that shrouded their forms. It was both destiny and magic. Even the breeze caressed them and the setting sun touched them with the glistening brilliance of a thousand diamonds; the earth knew it was right; she sheltered them; she embraced them benignly.

The cloak fell unnoticed from her fingers as they curled around the steellike pillar of his neck. First with awe, and then with fervor, her fingers explored him, the endless hardness of his back, the dark, thickly curled expanse of his chest. The cloak no longer separated them; she arched her breasts against his chest, scarcely able to breathe with the dizzying sensation created by the friction of her tautening nipples against that erotic hair and the blazing heat that filled him. And still that first kiss continued. He held her face tenderly between his hands, and then his hands began to move. They massaged her temple, raking through her damp hair. They found the column of her throat; his thumbs reverently touched upon the ivory silk.

Suddenly he broke the kiss—only to allow his lips to fall upon the blue-veined pulse that beat erratically beneath the touch of his thumb. His hands wandered over the clean slope of her shoulders, caressing the fine lines of her collarbones before heatedly discovering the full weight of her breasts. They were warm and giving; they arched to him, filling his hands, and he held them both tenderly and possessively while bringing his mouth to their hardened peaks and caressing that firmness with tongue and gentle teeth.

All that he could think was that she was pure aphrodisiac; unbelievably sweet; an essence of honey, the nectar of the gods. And he was either in heaven, or dreaming, because she was as passionately eager as he was insatiably hungry. It is bewitchment, he thought vaguely, and if he had been at all sane, he would have laughed at himself because he was a scientist and he had spent his life disproving such phenomena existed.

He could have kissed her forever, tasting that wonderful creamy flesh with its faint scent of roses. But the need in him was too tangible; it was a volcano, screaming within him to explode. Leaned against her as he was, his knee—such a contrast to hers, large and dark with the curled hair that also spanned his chest against her silky limb—wedged further. And like the petals of the rose that were her scent, her smooth thighs glided apart easily. It was a spell; at that point he was certain. She was in the grips of that spell as thoroughly as he. Poised between the long and lithe beauty of her legs, he quickly shed his cutoffs. He wanted to know her thoroughly, to make love forever with time standing still. He wanted to hear her speak, to watch her smile, to know her life . . . everything about her. It was a spell . . . the feeling of knowing each other, of knowing it was meant to be. He needed her now, to be within her, to let

17

that urgent desire find release within her . . . and he could see in her eyes that he did not imagine her responses.

She had become his, his to love, to know, to explore, to taunt to new heights each time they lay together.

Relieved of his restrictive clothing, he knelt between that ivory prison of shapely calves and thighs. He bent to take her lips once more; his hands spanned over her breasts, slid low over her abdomen, skimmed over the heart of her heat. He tore his mouth from hers; her lips were parted and wet from his; her eyes met his. They were misted, still incredulous, hauntingly mysterious, and yet openly giving.

He trailed his fingers lightly but firmly down the length of her inner thighs, taunting and loving, eliciting deeper sensation to heights that matched his own. She cried out at his touch, and a tremor raked through her. Her arms stretched out to him, encircling his neck, bringing her up to where she could bury her head against his neck. Firmly he brought her back to the earth; he entered her with a care that was quickly lost to spiraling passion. It was he who shuddered uncontrollably with that impact. She was sweetly moist, taking him into her with a feminine grace and a shivering, open need that was the most beautiful he had ever known.

He was the fire she had known he would be, and even as the urgent splendor of that storming passion took her higher to oblivious blue skies, she was still a bit in awe. Oh Lord, his size and his strength were awesome. When he had first knelt before her, it hadn't occurred to her at all that she was behaving indecently, that she should be ashamed of herself for falling into the arms of this stranger.

No, if she had been worried at all, she had been worried that she wouldn't prove woman enough to handle the pulse and strength of him. But his touch had been all the catalyst needed. She had welcomed him with deep-seated instinct; he filled her, making her insides feel like they would ignite momentarily, her mind delirious, blanketed by a silver cloud of shivering splendor. He had filled her, and she had embraced him with all the innate sensuality he had tapped.

She arched against him, moved with him in the undulations of her own raw need, welcoming each demanding velvet thrust, even as tempo increased wildly to skyrocketing, explosive proportions. She was vaguely aware that she moaned, that she cried out, that she raked her nails over his back and tore her fingers through his hair. But she was mainly aware that he touched her as she had never been touched before. He made her burn with the fire that was within her, catapulting her with driving, agonized hunger up and up so high.

She heard music, in the trees. And it blessed them as did the earth, with the thunderous beat of drums, the melody of flute and strings. It was hauntingly sweet; and its tune whispered that this was destiny; it was right, because such beauty had to be right.

The drums were the pounding of his heart, the whisper the sound of his uneven breath. The crescendo was her cry, mingled with his, as he imbedded himself deeply, filling her with the essence of him. Shudders attacked her in great racking waves as she acknowledged that she had never known such ecstasy, such volatile and ultimate fulfillment that belonged only very intimately between a man and a woman.

For several seconds they lay in a luxurious embrace, savoring that moment, but then, realizing his weight, he shifted, drawing her beside him. They were both content to hold the spell.

She lay against his chest, still mesmerized by its breadth, by the definition of each individual bulging muscle.

Funny, she had always told herself she didn't care for the muscled type. She thought an abundance of muscles was certainly ugly. But there was nothing ugly about him; his appeal was totally rugged, as if he did, indeed, swing a sword daily, fighting with power and cunning to survive.

His fingers, incredibly light for their length and size, gentled over her cheekbones. "Have you a name, beautiful seductress?" he inquired lightly. "Or are you an illusion?"

She laughed uneasily; speech, as she had feared, had broken the spell. He was still extraordinary, but she was suddenly beginning to realize what she had done.

"Not an illusion," she murmured, her soft, light tone hiding the nervousness she was feeling within. "A witch. This is Salem, remember? A place for witchcraft and magic."

"But I don't believe in magic," he told her.

"Don't you?" she murmured. "I assure you, it exists."

He laughed suddenly, and she liked the sound. It was deep and rich and full. "A white witch, I hope?"

"Of course," she replied, grateful that he was following the whimsy of the conversation. She had to get away from him, try to analyze what she had done. Dear God, but what could she do? Rise and say "Excuse me, I think I'll leave now"? He would never let her leave—like that. And reality told her now that they both had lives to return to; that a man such as this was very experienced; she had probably been one in a multitude who had fallen victim to his touch.

Except I doubt few fell as fast, she told herself scornfully, suddenly ashamed. Still, she had no intention of stupidly saying that she never did such things as she had obviously just done. He didn't believe in witchcraft—how could she explain that she had been under his spell and that it had just been so beautiful and right?

With her senses returned, she wasn't even believing the situation herself. But she was lying naked beside a man as splendidly formed as a knight of medieval times and his fingers were still caressing her naked flesh and she was still savoring that touch.

Face it, she had just made love with some jock weight lifter, and where on earth did one go from there, especially when confusion was now her reigning emotion?

He was watching her; those deep hazel eyes were reading her too clearly.

"Was there a reason," he demanded quietly, "that you shouldn't have made love with me? A husband? A fiancé?"

"No," she said with a furious blush. "I mean yes." Of course there was a reason; she simply didn't do things like this . . . remotely like this . . . and, dear God, now he was really staring at her, assuming from her confused answer that she not only did do things like this but that she was a married woman who did things like this. . . . "I mean, no, I'm not married. . . ."

His grin slowly returned as he rose to sit, still eyeing her nakedness possessively. "Good," he said lightly.

She frowned in sudden horror. "Are you married?"

He laughed again, that throaty sound that sent provocative tingles racing down her spine. "No, witch, I assure you, I'm not married."

He bent to brush her lips with a kiss. "Believe it or not," he said ruefully, "I happen to have some wine. Would you like some?"

Her brows lifted in query, and he pointed across the pond to a cooler beneath an oak. "Ah, yes, please," she murmured. If he went for the wine, she could escape.

But he clutched her hands as he rose and drew her to her feet, cradling her body against his. She shivered again with the electric contact; it was incredible how intensely she could feel him, how his flesh, even now, burned hers, how it made her dizzy, ready to fall against him and accept his touch all over.

"Come on," he murmured, and he set off toward the water with her hand firmly grasped within his. Totally disoriented simply by the feel of his body against hers, she followed without protest. He was comfortable, completely unselfconscious of his own nakedness. He wouldn't allow her to be self-conscious of her own . . . and after the way she had responded to him, it would surely be absurd for her to profess modesty now.

But just before they reached the opposite shore, he swept her into his arms again. And there, in the water that reached her midriff, he made love to her again, and once he touched her, she felt powerless to stop him. His attraction was undeniable; she couldn't attempt to lie to either him or herself. He turned to take her hand, laughing with the devil in his eyes, and bent to kiss. And then his hands cradled her buttocks, lifting her, and she was once more lost to the delirium of his demanding sensuality.

But when he procured the small splits of wine, she laughingly insisted they return to her side of the shore. And as she employed all her wiles to keep from any serious discussion, she feigned a growing exhaustion, until she once more lay against his massive chest wishing that they could speak seriously, that she could invite him home to dinner, that she could get to know him, that she could have him forever.

But she had a man, a very good and decent man, and if he wasn't already at the inn, he would be there soon. And even if she didn't know whether she loved him or not, she could never appear before him suddenly with another man. She owed Marc a certain loyalty.

Loyalty! She laughed bitterly to herself. Loyalty! I have been with a man twice whose name I don't know, and the only excuse I can come up with is a spell?

Her face flooded red with shame, yet still she couldn't regret the experience. She had never known passion like that before. It had been destiny they should meet, that she should learn just how rapturously beautiful it could be to be with a man.

She suddenly discovered she was crying as she lay against his chest. How she had needed him. Perhaps that had been part of the spell. And it had all happened so quickly.

With the tears sliding silently down her cheeks, she continued to feign sleep. She felt the subtle change in his chest when he too dozed. I can run now, she thought, but I don't think I can ever escape this encounter.

Her eyes closed as she rested with him, waiting for his sleep to become deep. But then her wait became her own downfall; comfortable, uniquely secure and sweetly exhausted, she slept. When she awoke, darkness had almost thoroughly descended. Only the moon's glitter upon the pond shed light.

She was alone; her cloak lay around her shoulders.

She jolted to a sitting position, staring around her. There was nothing, no sign of human habitation other than herself.

Shivering, she strained her eyes across the pond. There was no sign of a man with the naked beauty of a barbarian . . . no sign of anything.

Mystified, she covered her eyes with her hands and groaned. Was I dreaming? She blushed with the thought; surely it was impossible to dream anything so erotic, so full of thought and detail . . . ?

Or am I seeing things?

I've gone crazy. I must have gone crazy.

"Oh, God!" she groaned aloud, clenching her teeth. Which would be better? she wondered bitterly: to convince herself she was losing her mind and envisioning things, or realize and accept the fact that she had just made love with a total stranger?

She began to shake. No, she told herself. He had been real. He had been wearing cutoffs. He had offered her wine in twentieth century splits. No one could imagine, or envision, or dream such an interlude.

Marc would tell her that she was recalling things, emotions from the past, that she had been having insight and adding the contemporary pieces with her mind. Marc was the one who believed in spells and ghosts and strange quirks of the mind. He would tell her that she had dreamed up someone's tumultuous past.

Marc. The man she was dating. The man she supposedly cared for.

She could never tell Marc about this!

If she had been dreaming, she assured herself, it had been a normal dream—one a psychiatrist might have a heyday with—but otherwise normal.

It was dark. They were supposed to be in Boston by ten, and she was late.

She jumped to her feet, drawing her cloak about her. Even without the moonlight, she would have found the almost invisible path between the trees. She started running.

She stumbled, gasping. Her eyes turned upward; a full moon rode the sky.

Witches' moon was what they called it.

She choked back a little cry and started running once more through the woods she knew so well.

Soon she reached her home, entering the inn by the rear "false" door and following the hidden staircase, Eleanora's staircase, to her room. She had barely closed the door behind her and started to run her bath when she heard a gentle tap at the door.

"Serena," Martha Heyer, her housekeeper, chef, and all-around friend and confidante, called softly. "Marc is here."

"Thanks, Martha!" Serena called out, willing her teeth not to chatter. "Tell him just a few minutes."

"Sure thing, sweetie," Martha returned. "But he seems mighty nervous about this dinner. I'd hurry if I were you."

"I'll hurry."

The bath water was running. Serena rushed to her dresser to pull out the black chemise and slip she would wear with the filmy black cocktail dress. Absently she pulled the ribbon of her cloak and it fell to the floor.

She started to move hurriedly away from the dresser when she was suddenly caught by her reflection in the mirror above it.

There was a tiny reddened patch above her left breast, and as she stared at it, she noticed two more, one on her right hip, one on her upper right thigh.

The mirror also reflected her color as she turned rose-red from head to toe. She hadn't been dreaming; the man had been no apparition. Not unless apparitions had substance.

But she had known she hadn't been dreaming. Unless she had also dreamed that pleasant male scent that still lingered about her, that feeling of being passionately cherished, deliciously loved.

She tore away from the mirror and hurriedly plunged into the bath. But she bit her lip furiously as she hesitated before purging her flesh thoroughly with her own rosewood soap.

And she had to stop and remind herself that time was of the essence as she found herself staring out the skylight and noticing once more that a full moon rode the heavens.

A witches' moon.

CHAPTER ONE

The highway had become a continuous ribbon of gray and black. Justin blinked, trying to dispel the illusion. A bead of perspiration dripped from a dark thick brow into his eye, and he blinked furiously once more, then sighed. He hadn't planned to stop until he reached the town and the guesthouse, but he had no suicidal tendencies nor did he intend his own tired driving to possibly injure another person. Besides, his long legs seemed cramped as all hell, and despite the air conditioning blasting through the small sports car, the July sun was creating an uncomfortable heat.

He pulled off the road, cut the engine, and immediately stepped out of the driver's side to stretch his cramped limbs.

Hands on hips he viewed his surroundings. He stood on an embankment of high grass beside that endless ribbon of highway. He had been driving without a stop, except to fill the gas tank, since he had left New York City, and now he had begun to succumb to road mesmerization.

Actually, he thought with a deep, throaty chuckle that startled a few birds from the trees, he couldn't be more than a few miles from his destination—Salem. If he had just been able to hold out a few minutes more.

No, it felt too good to be out of the car, and the forestry that surrounded the road on either side seemed to lend a certain coolness to the oppressive July heat. And hell, there was no fire he had to get to. He was his own boss and therefore had all the time in the world. He shrugged a little ruefully to himself. The city had taught him to hurry; life was high-speed, spiral gear. And he had to admit he was a perfect candidate for the pace of the city. He was a bit of a workaholic—and when he wasn't working, he was still going, moving, doing.

Justin stretched once more and started to fold his legs back into the confines of the car, but then hesitated. His deep hazel eyes were caught by the movement and rustle of the maple and oak trees that grew densely along the side of the road. A breeze was lilting through the branches, and the gentle sway of the foliage was as mesmerizing as the road. A crooked grin split the strong line of his jaw. The eyes that had appeared so deep and intense were suddenly lit with a twinkling brilliance as he laughed at himself. I'm being compelled by those trees, he thought with a grimace. No, not by the trees, but by a need to relax, to feel the breeze or the touch of a leaf.

He had been driving barefoot; he reached into the car for a pair of leather sandals, then slammed the door shut and locked as he balanced himself with a hand on the roof of the car while he slid his feet into the sandals. Whistling softly, he strode around to the trunk, inserted the key, and popped it open to secure a small Playmate cooler. Then he started toward the trees and the certain area that had especially attracted his attention—a break in the trees that indicated a small footpath.

The trail was overgrown, obviously no longer still in use. It was cool beneath the sheltering leaves, and he could smell the earth and the greenery. There had to be a lake or lagoon within the forestry, he thought, to give the area its intensely fresh and crisp feeling despite the summer heat. Good place to jog, he thought almost mechanically, glad he had stopped driving because he would certainly return.

He followed the break in the trees, and as he had expected, the clearing portrayed a body of water, still and clear, reflecting the sun with a crystal brilliance like a bed of sparkling diamonds. His footsteps quickened until he reached the end of the trees, then he slowed, appreciating the view of the water and the tall grasses that grew to its edge, giving way to soft, sandy dirt. The breeze stirred suddenly, causing the grass to bend and dip as if in supplication, and seeming to kiss his forehead with coolness while lifting a thatch of dark hair from his brow. He dropped the cooler beside a tree and stripped his knit kelly sport shirt over his head to relish the coolness against a broad, heavily muscled chest. Then, like a kid at a watering hole, he whooped out a joyous cry and pelted into the water, sinewed calves and rock-hard thighs moving him at a wild, breakneck pace.

The water was actually cold. It hit his flesh with a delightful shock, and he swam steadily through it. Reaching the middle, he doubled and headed toward the bottom—it was no more than twenty-five feet deep—and was surprised and pleased to discover nothing but rocks or sand. No beer or soda cans—not even an old boot. The small pond was as clean and natural as the foliage that harbored it.

Minutes later he swam back to the shore, shivering slightly as the air hit his flesh, but loving the sensation. After all the heat, it was wonderful.

He walked a few feet from the water to sit beneath the tree that sheltered his cooler. He grimaced as his wallet creaked beneath him—he had forgotten he carried it in the back pocket of his cutoffs. He half rose, pulled out his wallet and a few waterlogged bills, and set them beside him on a large flat rock that seemed to be attracting a few rays of the sunshine that filtered through the trees. Then he dug a beer out of the cooler, popped it open, and leaned back against the trunk of the tree. Damn, but it felt good to be alone. It felt especially good to be away from Denise.

He winced and closed his eyes at the unbidden thought. There wasn't a thing wrong with Denise. She was beautiful, sophisticated, intelligent—and one hell of a determined lover. A little too determined, he thought with a frown, bothered that he should be feeling any guilt. He had told her from the beginning that he didn't believe in marriage and was essentially a loner. And Denise, liberated woman that she claimed to be, assured him that she certainly didn't intend to marry either—why would she want to become some man's maid?

But she seemed a little too fond of his position, of the prestige that came with each of his acclaimed books.

Face it, Justin told himself with a certain amount of disgust, you're here just as much because of Denise as because of any desire to do thorough research.

Not just Denise, but my entire life-style.

Denise was so fond of the things he was coming to wish he could avoid. She loved the faculty lunches, the dinners, the cocktail parties. And she adored autograph parties. She was so gracious . . . so gracious that he was sometimes sure that he could see the wheels of her mind turning within the emerald glitter of her eyes. Predatory eyes. She was a brilliant and cunning woman, certain that in claiming her own freedom, she would eventually bring him around to where he believed he needed her.

He lifted his beer can to the powder-blue sky and the liquid brilliance of the sun. "Keep shining like that," he assured the golden orb, "and you will convince me that I'm a country boy at heart!"

He dated other women, and he didn't hide the fact from Denise. She allowed him that freedom too, and that was a little of what bothered him. She should have been perfect: she was the toast of all his friends, and despite his wandering ways, he was well aware that she remained loyal. That too bothered him. It was all so calculated. No real emotion. Like he sometimes felt about her lovemaking. Well-planned, well-practiced mechanics. Anything to please.

He shrugged and sipped his beer. Maybe he should marry her. He could settle down and have two point five children and vacation on the Riviera every year. He was assured the presidency of the university in another ten years. Denise would never run to fat—she was too egotistical ever to do so. She would always be perfect, his house neat as a pin, his two point five children would wear clothing without a dot of dirt or hint of a wrinkle. Surely a man could meet a fate far worse than that.

No. He had been married before. For all of two years. To a woman just as beautiful and just as perfect. And from that relationship had come one good thing, a daughter who spent exactly one month with him every year, and then every other Christmas vacation.

It wasn't that he didn't believe in love, he simply didn't believe in love lasting. It began so beautifully, but time made caricatures of love; it became contorted, buried beneath jealousy, spite, and all those other things that raised their ugly heads as disagreements mounted steadily to shouting matches.

He finished his beer and smiled to himself. Nine out of ten times he blamed himself for the problems in his relationships. He was a man who needed space as well as being someone who didn't really know how to give. Mary and he had been a disaster from the start. They had married out of high school because she had been pregnant—ironically, she had lost the baby. The relationship had been shaky, but she had gotten pregnant again right away, and he had been bound to stay, bound to try. But the daughter who should have strengthened their love merely became a pathetic pawn in the shouting matches. Money had been their basic problem. He had been a struggling student himself in those days. And there had been a few too many older men around to take Mary to dinner when he couldn't or when he was studying. Maybe, he told himself, he had never forgiven her for accepting those invitations behind his back, for turning "dinners" into affairs.

Justin yawned and rested the back of his head against the tree. At the moment, he thought with a smile, he would give his eyeteeth for something uncomplicated. The pond was so wild and welcoming—and secluded. It should be shared, he thought. A wood nymph should slip out of the trees and he should wildly attack her—only to discover that she welcomed his touch and had provoked the attack.

He laughed aloud at his thoughts. This was Salem, he reminded himself dryly. Land of witches—not wood nymphs. And as dean of the Department of Clinical Psychology at one of New York State's most prestigious colleges, he was here to study the result of natural human phenomena—not crystal balls and spells and incantations.

But at that moment, it was more fun not to be Professor O'Neill. It was enjoyable to believe that the trees had created a little slice of heaven for him. He folded his long fingers and broad hands behind his head and sighed with that delicious feeling of being alone with the caress of the breeze, the feel of the dirt beneath him, and the freedom to laugh at his own ridiculous fantasies.

He slept, and then dreamed. But it was only when he awoke that he lived out a fantasy that became real.

And awaking the second time was even better. His arms were around his ivory witch; she slept peacefully upon his chest. He adjusted himself to stare down at her with a twisted smile easing the lines of strain about his eyes. She was warm and sweetly lovely as she lay against him, long fingers splayed over the dark curls on his chest. Chestnut hair, now dry and silky, tangled over his limbs.

She was unlike any woman he had ever known—completely natural, giving unselfconsciously, receiving with simple, unabashed pleasure. Nor was there anything of the hardened expert about her; he felt as if he had tapped a crystal innocence and found the depths of sensuality that lurked beneath the fragile shield.

Who the hell was she? he wondered. He had to know—he was so curious he almost woke her. But her lips were parted in a curving smile—he couldn't break her sleep. He had all the time in the world. And she must live near—how else could she appear at the pond with only a cloak?

The summer was beginning to look promising indeed.

He ran a finger over her face, noticed its softness, then its chill. Frowning, he eased her head to the ground, then walked the few feet to her cape to secure it protectively around her. He watched her for another moment with curious tenderness, then stood and stretched and slipped back into his cutoffs. He glanced around, and it occurred to him how dark it was getting. Thank God there was a full moon or he wouldn't be able to see his hand before his face. He paused for a moment, looking down at her, decided she was deeply asleep, and thought that he'd hurry back to the car for his huge lantern—he wanted a little light on the subject when she awoke and he quizzed her.

He walked around the pond this time, absently picked up the split bottles and the cooler, and stumbled back through the trail that had brought him.

Except that going back in the dark was a hell of a lot harder than coming had been.

He cursed himself for an idiot as he lost his way through the trees, muttering beneath his breath as leaves slapped his face. What a woodsman! he thought with a groan. But eventually he found the car—bright and shiny beneath the moonlight. He replaced the cooler and threw the garbage on the floor of the passenger seat, then scrounged around in the trunk until he found his massive flashlight.

Returning to the pond once more was a hell of a lot easier with the light. He began to wonder about her again as he walked, a little in awe of the whole situation. Women—no, he admitted fairly, not just women, but people—usually had motives. Most of the time, they wanted something.

That was part of what had been so unique. They had met, touched, and come together. The meeting was as unique as the woman. And as he had never been before, he was anxious to find out about her.

And he was anxious to hold her again. He was already wondering if anything could have been so damned good . . . or had it just been the twilight, playing tricks upon his senses?

When he reached the pond again, he incredulously discovered that she was gone. Vanished. Without a trace.

He felt as if he were a madman—rushing about the place like an idiot, searching the foliage high and low, then standing there like a fool with his light trained upon the water.

31

She simply wasn't there. Not a sign of her. The entire interlude might not have been.

As he stared at the water, a horror engulfed him. What if she hadn't felt so wonderful about the experience? He didn't know a damned thing about her. She might be mentally unbalanced. She might have . . .

He dropped the flashlight and dove into the water, surfaced, dove again. Over and over, until he had covered—as best he could in the darkness—the entire pond.

Then he got up to sit by the shoreline, feeling even more like an idiot—and more furious.

Now if he found her, he wanted to throttle her!

He panted to regain his breath after his efforts and finally puffed out an exasperated sigh. Incredible. It appeared now as if he sat before nothing more than a dark pond. Nothing could have happened here. His experience with a witch at twilight might have been a date with magic.

He stood with an impatient grumble. He didn't believe in magic—and his witch had been a flesh and blood woman. And he would find her even if it meant searching not just Salem, but all of Massachusetts.

Muttering disgustedly to himself, he started back for the car a second time. He found his way easily with the flashlight; but he felt uncomfortable because his clothes were sopping wet; his green Izod dripped on his cutoffs which in turn dripped on his sandals and his bare toes.

He was muttering as he drove into Salem—only to discover that he hadn't read his map well. The road he should have been on ran parallel to the one he had taken. He had to backtrack to find the inn, wondering all the while how the proprietress would greet a soaking wet guest.

But the smiling, middle-aged woman who answered the door merely clucked over his appearance, warning him that while July days were hot in Salem, the nights could become very cool. She ushered him into a warm parlor while promising hot coffee and towels. He had to duck to enter the parlor—the room was part of the original house and built with a low ceiling.

"You'll have to forgive a few idiosyncrasies, Dr. O'Neill," the woman offered with a cheerful smile. "We only let out three rooms, you know, and we don't operate like a regular guesthouse. Breakfast is promptly at eight, lunch at noon, and dinner at six. And I'd appreciate it if you would let me know when you intend to miss meals—but on the other hand, if you have a special preference, you let me know, and I'll get it on the table for you. I'm afraid your room has a bath but no shower, and you'll find a few other inconveniences—"

"Please!" Justin laughed. "I know all about the Golden Hawk—and that's why I'm here." He smiled. "If you'll just let me know what to call you, ma'am—"

"Oh! I'm Martha, Martha Heyer."

"Mrs. Heyer, I'll be as happy as a lark here, I assure you."

"Martha," Martha corrected, as awed by the man's smile as by his tight, muscular build. He looked far more like a gladiator than a professor, of all things. She smiled to herself in return. She had assumed Dr. Justin O'Neill would be a stooped old man with bifocals and a cane.

"Oh!" Martha muttered suddenly, handing him a cup of coffee from a pewter pot that sat over a small woodburning stove. "Dear me, Dr. O'Neill! I forgot with you coming in dripping wet and all! I've a message for you. From a lady says her name is Denise! She called hours ago—we did expect you earlier—and asked that I tell you she was flying into Boston—wants to meet you at the Sheraton. Dinner at ten o'clock. But if you can't make it, no problem. She'll drive out here—"

"Oh, hell!" Justin muttered, forgetting Martha for a moment. Then he glanced at her to apologize. "Sorry, but could I have my room key?" He glanced at his watch. Nine twenty. Twenty minutes for a shower, no, bath, twenty minutes to make it back to Boston. But he had to make it. Damn, what was she doing following him out here? He had made it clear he wanted the summer alone to work.

Denise would probably have some good reason for being in Boston.

33

And he probably wouldn't be feeling so antagonistic if it hadn't been for his meeting with a witch at a pond.

But even though he was ready to throttle that nameless witch, he was haunted by her. She had been uniquely special, and suddenly, he felt as if he could settle for nothing less. He had to find out first if that feeling was real; if she had been as warm and giving as memory now decreed and if the fever she had left in his blood truly existed.

"Thank you." He was leaving as Martha Heyer handed him his keys, explaining that one was to the front door, the other to his room. He grimaced at the woman. "I guess I'm going to have to hurry to make a ten o'clock appointment."

"Don't drive too fast!" Martha warned. "No appointment is worth a life!"

"No." Justin smiled. "I won't drive too fast."

"Your room is just left at the top of the stairs." Martha smiled, feeling a little foolish that she instinctively liked the man so. "Feel free to raid the refrigerator or make use of the kitchen or the parlor when you return. I retire a bit early, but we like our guests to feel at home. Just be careful about wandering around—the house has a few tricks to it!"

"So I've heard," Justin returned, setting his coffee cup down and ducking as he passed Martha to head for the main stairway. "I'm anxious to hear all about it. Perhaps you'll give me some history tomorrow."

"That's right, you're a writer, eh?"

"Professor, not really a writer. Not as in the sense of the classics. I'm doing a book on the psychology of the witchcraft trials."

"Oh, I see," Martha murmured, but she didn't really see at all. She shook her head slightly. He didn't look the type to be at all bookish. But Salem attracted all kinds.

"Well, anyway, Dr. O'Neill," Martha offered, "you talk to Serena in the morning. She's the one knows all about the place. Oh—and incidentally, she runs a little museum you might enjoy."

"Serena?" He wasn't really listening anymore; he was in a

34

hurry to get upstairs, bathe and dress and get back to Boston to find out what Denise was up to before he wound up with his summer a nightmare.

"Umm, Mrs. Loren—she owns the place. You just missed her —but like I said, you'll meet her in the morning. Whatever you're up to, I'm sure she'll be able to help."

"Thank you again, Martha," Justin said quickly, bumping his head on the low ceiling as he hurried to reach the stairway. "I'm sure I will get a lot from . . . Serena."

He didn't have much time to appreciate the beautiful lines of the old house, or the history captured in its architecture as he reached his room, tossed down his cases, and ran his bath. He barely noticed that all the furnishings were authentic antiques; yet he did appreciate the little hospitalities, such as fresh flowers in a vase, a note of welcome in a feminine hand, and towels in the bath that smelled of sunshine rather than a laundry.

Tomorrow, he would get into the spirit of the thing, but now . . .

His anger grew as he bathed and dressed in a casual tweed dinner jacket. Denise was manipulating him—and yet, he shouldn't really be angry with Denise. He had kept the affair going.

But tonight, of all nights, he didn't want to see her. He wanted to savor the magic, the magic he didn't believe in.

"I'm going to find that woman!" he growled aloud.

And then he laughed at himself. More than likely, he'd never see her again, no matter how strong his determination. He had no right to behave cruelly to Denise because he had been spurned by a mystery witch.

When he dealt with Denise, he wanted to do so honestly. He wanted her to understand his feelings, to respect them. He had always been honest. He could only give her so much, and if it wasn't enough, then that was that.

But when he left his room, he could have sworn he sensed a smell of roses. And he couldn't get that incredibly erotic and yet innocent vision of his white witch out of his mind. The memory of her ivory skin sleek and glistening as she stretched to embrace the twilight lingered.

And as he revved his car into gear again, he was once more muttering that he would find "that damned woman," and when he did, he would certainly either throttle her, or tan her bewitching rear!

But he didn't believe in witchcraft—his witch was real, she was flesh and blood. And what she gave was real; he had never known a woman so sensual, so sweetly innocent yet fully passionate. And they hadn't yet begun to really explore a half of the intimacies awaiting them.

There was no pretense about her, he thought wryly; that was a part of her ultimate beauty.

His lips went thin across his jaw as he thought about her swift vanishing act, but he knew he would find her.

CHAPTER TWO

"Serena, Jerry was talking to you."

Jolted back to the present, Serena Loren was greeted by a stern frown from her escort, Marc Talbot. She met his suspiciously narrowed eyes with guilt twisting at her heart, then quickly glanced to the third party at their dinner party, Jerry Kloon, Marc's publisher. She smiled uneasily and hastily apologized. "I'm sorry, Jerry, I'm afraid I simply blanked there for a moment. What were you saying?"

"I asked what you thought of Marc's idea, Serena," the handsome older man with silver hair and beard of the same color said with a small, understanding smile. "The inn does belong to you."

"Oh," Serena said uneasily, drawing her eyes from Jerry's to stare at her water glass. She ran a manicured finger idly over the crystal rim as she stalled for a little time. Then she smiled back to Jerry. "I have great faith in Marc's work," she said sincerely. "I think he'll do just fine."

Kloon smiled down at his own plate, admiring the evasive poise of the uniquely arresting woman with whom he conversed. Her sense of loyalty would not allow her to dispute Marc, but Kloon was well aware that she didn't support Marc's theories, despite the fact that her replies were as smooth as the elegant column of her throat and the clean lines of her lovely face.

"That's not quite what I asked," Jerry Kloon said, carefully dabbing his distinguished handlebar mustache with the corner of his napkin. "Do you believe that the Golden Hawk houses ghosts, spooks, poltergeists, or other entities of the night?"

She wished she would have worn her hair down so that she might hide behind it. She wished she would have been paying attention to the previous conversation. She wished she would have been on time, so that Marc wasn't half prepared to strangle her already.

She wished desperately she could explain to herself what had happened earlier so that she didn't now feel so incredibly bewildered when it was so terribly important she speak intelligently.

"I think that Marc will be able to create a marvelous book!" she said with enthusiasm. "There are fantastic stories that go with the history of the inn! The wife of an eighteenth century sea captain is claimed to prowl the widow's walk—and they did find the bones of a young girl sealed into one of the hidden stairways! It's said that she was accused of witchcraft during the 1692 trials, and that her husband, a ferociously jealous man, swore to protect her, but believed her guilty not of witchcraft, but adultery, and therefore sealed her to her fate! The legends that surround the place are really marvelous!" Serena finished speaking, and quickly picked up her wineglass to take a long sip. Her heart was thudding painfully as she prayed Jerry Kloon would allow the subject to drop. Marc, she knew, was desperate to do the book. And at the moment, she was so guilt-ridden that there was nothing she wanted to see more than Marc happy and secure.

Kloon didn't intend to let the matter rest. He lifted a brow high in skepticism. "But I take it you don't believe in haunts yourself, Serena, nor ghosts of any kind."

Serena flushed uneasily. "I don't see where my beliefs are relevant, Mr. Kloon," she murmured. "What is important is how competently a writer can deal with the legends."

Kloon shrugged his brows noncommittally, and Marc, his

brown eyes now anxious, jumped into the pause. "Don't let Serena fool you with her blasé appearance, sir. I believe she's afraid of her own perception—she has ESP, you know."

"Oh, is that true?" Kloon cast a piercing stare Serena's way.

Serena wanted to kick Marc. "I don't believe I actually have ESP, sir, no more so than the average person, at any rate. I have a brother ten months younger than I am. We were very close growing up, and we can sometimes sense things about each other. Most close siblings have that ability."

"You never know," Kloon said. He tapped his fingers upon the snow-white linen tablecloth, apparently deep in thought. "Well," he said, glancing from one anxious face to the other, "would you care for dessert or a liqueur? Or perhaps you would like to stroll with me back to my hotel? They have a lovely little lounge that specializes in South Seas concoctions—piña-coladas they serve in ceramic coconuts, something marvelous with dry ice that puffs and sizzles and the like."

Serena opened her mouth to decline. It was growing very late, and as well as the Golden Hawk itself, she had another business to run, one that required her presence bright and early.

"I'd like to try one of those smoking things," Marc said eagerly, casting a warning eye Serena's way. "And we have to walk back to the hotel anyway. My car is in the garage."

Kloon signaled for the check; Serena tried to appear enthusiastic rather than tired as they left the restaurant behind, taking one last glance at the magnificent view of the Boston streets from the top of the Prudential. Serena became quickly aware from Marc's rough escorting touch that he was less than pleased with her comments. The walk from the Prudential to the Sheraton lounge seemed interminably long.

I couldn't lie to him, Marc, she pleaded silently. He would have known I was lying, and that would have been much worse.

Suddenly corridors and columns and glass merged before her, and she was drifting again. It wasn't Marc who touched her, but *him*, and it was that marvelous feeling of being exactly where she belonged, as if she had known a thousand years. She

39

was secure; there was nothing to compare with the security of his complete possession.

But then that euphoria drifted away; a flush of blood suffused her cheeks, and she felt weak and horrified with shame. It couldn't have really happened; surely it had been a dream. Dear God, she was a nice person, and nice people simply didn't do things like that.

A new horror hit her at that moment. Salem was small; too small. Most visitors were tourists, and she ran a tourist attraction. There was more than a sound possibility that she would run into the man somewhere. She had been so concerned with hiding her own identity, she hadn't bothered to discover his.

He was just passing through, she tried to assure herself. And *mine certainly isn't the biggest tourist attraction; I'm being ridiculous, I will never see him again.*

Oh, Lord, what must he think of me?

And then she was angry, wondering why she should have to feel such terrible guilt and humiliation. He probably didn't feel a thing—men were supposed to be able to do macho things like instantly hop into bed—or earth, as the case might be—on a moment's notice. But a woman! No, no, no! That made her terrible.

I would have thought it terrible myself until today.

"Serena!"

She felt her arm gripped sharply and realized she had made a complete circumference through the revolving glass doors.

"I brought you to help!" Marc hissed in her ear. "And first you make us late—then you won't support me. And now I'm not even sure you're with us anymore!"

"I'm sorry, I'm sorry!" Serena murmured quickly, forcing a quick and overly radiant smile to her lips as she noticed Kloon over Marc's shoulder watching their interlude with a dry, suppressed grin. She hurried her steps to match with the men's, keeping that smile plastered to her face. "I do love a good piña-colada, Mr. Kloon," she said easily. Kloon was an extremely pleasant man; it was no difficulty to enjoy his company; she was simply finding the situation difficult.

"Ahhh, Serena, I thought you might have gone for the smoking brew. I understand that you run a witchcraft museum and shop. Are you a practicing witch yourself?"

Serena laughed. "No, Mr. Kloon, I do not practice witchcraft, but I have a number of customers who do! All white witches, to the best of my knowledge." Her smile became more serious. "Witchcraft is a very important business in Salem these days. The city survives off the tourism—and off our good witches! These days, the practices are a lot like any other belief in the raising of the conscious—" She paused and shrugged at a lack of words for the explanation she needed. "Something like yoga, or Tai Chi, or meditation! The women I know who are involved care about nature, herbs and plants and animals—and people! And being the best that they can be!"

"You come on well in their defense," Kloon observed as they entered the lounge, a pretty place with a well-done South Seas flavor.

"Of course." Serena laughed. "I'm not a fool!"

She glanced at Marc, who now seemed pleased with her as he smiled and pulled out a chair, seating her silently before pulling his own chair close.

"Serena is a wealth of knowledge." Marc laughed. "She's almost like having a living and breathing encyclopedia."

A waitress appeared; drinks were ordered. As the menu promised, they arrived steaming and frothing, and the threesome laughed as they tried to keep talking through the slowly diminishing haze. But the haze reminded her of the mist that night had brought to the pond, and she discovered that she was wandering once more.

"Serena really tells the story better."

She glanced at Marc blankly with horror. He took a deep breath and said with impatience lying just below his pleasant tone, "Eleanora, Serena."

"Oh . . . ah . . ." She took a sip of her drink and harshly warned herself to stop daydreaming and to pay attention. "There really aren't too many records available on her—just the notation that she was among the accused who disappeared

41

and that she was nineteen at the time, the wife of a certain John Hawk, first owner of the Golden Hawk. He was more than twice her age, but it wasn't unusual at that time for a young girl to be married to an older man of means. Anyway, John was terribly in love with her, but long before the witchcraft trials began, he had begun to suspect her of adultery. He took to following her each time she would leave the house." Serena hesitated only a moment, then continued, "He discovered that she did have a lover, a sea captain she had stumbled into at the pond near her house. He had been watering his horse, or some such thing, while looking for land. Legend has it that he was young and handsome and charismatic and strong—all things that the elderly Hawk certainly wasn't. And he fell head over heels in love with Eleanora. The two lovers made plans to run away. But Eleanora was accused of witchcraft. It's believed her husband secretly instigated the charge. Eleanora was terrified—several had already been hanged at the time—and with her lover away on the last voyage before their intended escape together, the poor lady turned to her husband, who pretended a desire to save her. He told her she must hide in the hidden staircase, and that when the house was searched it would be believed that she had already fled.

"When the sea captain returned, John Hawk informed him that Eleanora had fled with another man. Betrayed and desolate, the sea captain was beset by other trials: as Eleanora's known lover, he was accused of witchcraft before he could escape to his ship. Chained in his jail cell, he became desperately ill with a strange malady. He died, deliriously cursing his treacherous mistress, swearing he would find his vengeance." Serena lifted her hands in a poignant shrug. "Eleanora's bones weren't discovered until almost a century later—when the stairwell was broken into by a grandson of Hawk and Eleanora during the Revolutionary War in order to hide certain leaders when a British attack was believed imminent."

Serena lifted a brow delicately in Mr. Kloon's direction. "She is known, of course, to be the inn's most vocal haunt. There is a strong rumor that her screams echo through the stairwells. She does make a perfect ghost, don't you think, Mr. Kloon? A beautiful young girl betrayed by husband and peers and bereft of a lover?"

Kloon laughed. "A wonderful sales pitch, Serena. A romantic and tragic story. I believe—"

Suddenly, Serena wasn't listening any more. She had lifted her eyes from Kloon, and they had fallen across the room.

On a man.

Tall and dark and elegantly but ruggedly distinguished as he entered the lounge with a stunning brunette on his arm.

She barely noted the woman.

She was too shocked at seeing the man.

He wore the casual dinner jacket beautifully; he was terribly broad of shoulders with trim hips and waist. Even at a distance she could feel the power that radiated from his most simple flicker of movement. He looked completely at ease, and yet he looked as if he could suddenly rise and toss over the heavy wooden tables in a fit of primitive anger.

What a stupid thought. He was laughing as he bent his head to hear something the woman was saying. He appeared totally civil, even tempered, and alert with those deep crystal eyes sparkling in the dim light.

It was just that she knew what lurked beneath that elegant shield of evening attire. Flesh and blood and sinew . . . ruggedly, roughly, beautifully combined.

He didn't need to look her way. Even while her mind pleaded that it couldn't be, she knew that it was. Shocking that her jock weight lifter could appear so at ease and intellectual and charming; but he could . . . he most certainly could. . . .

"Serena!"

It was not Marc who called her name with concern this time, but Jerry Kloon. She heard him, but she didn't seem to be able to tear her eyes away from the apparition turned real before them.

"Serena . . ."

She fought as if from a swirl of mist. Her lips moved, but she

43

couldn't evoke sound. She closed her eyes, forcing herself to snap out of the horrified shock.

"I—I really am terribly sorry," she stammered to both Marc and Jerry. "I must be overtired tonight. . . ."

"It's the story," Marc was saying suddenly. "I shouldn't have had her tell you that story, Jerry. I told you she has a sense of ESP—I believe that she can feel for Eleanora, that she actually picks up the emotions and horrors of the past. If she ever chose to concentrate, she could probably see those lovers at the pond."

It was all she could do to keep from breaking into hysterical laughter. Oh, Marc, you are an absolute fool. I'm not feeling a thing in the world except for a sense of humiliation that's about to explode me into a million tiny pieces. And, oh, Marc, I can close my eyes and see lovers, and that's why I think I want to die at this particular second.

Serena coughed and took a sip of her drink. "Marc, please!" she said aloud. "I'm fine, I'm really just fine. Just tired," she murmured brightly.

"Shall we leave?" Kloon asked solicitously.

Marc stared at her pleadingly. An agreement hadn't been met yet.

I can't sit here! He could turn around; he could glance my way.

Marc's hand met hers under the table. Squeezed. He needed this deal. She was torn again with terrible guilt. She supposedly cared for Marc, and even if she hadn't as yet decided how deeply, as a friend she should be helping.

I can't sit here, Marc. You don't understand. And if you did, you really wouldn't understand. They had been dating almost a year; they had shared kisses and touches and warm evenings and days at the beach. They had come close to being lovers, and yet she had always drawn away, not certain that she could begin such a relationship so soon.

So soon.

If he ever knew, he would think her the worst hypocrite in the world. How could she ever explain what she didn't understand herself? I didn't know his name, but something was there that was natural, inevitable, right . . . destiny, magic, I don't know.

How ridiculous it all sounded in her mind.

Oh, Marc, I'm sorry; you deserved more from a woman than that.

She forced a smile and dipped her head to finish her drink. "I'm fine, really, and I'd just love another one of these!"

"Great," Jerry Kloon said agreeably. "We'll order another round."

Jerry and Marc began talking. Serena was vaguely aware that they were beginning to discuss terms, and she was thrilled—but then panicked.

The first time the men's steaming drinks had arrived at the table, the entire room had turned to laugh and speculate.

The incredibly real weight lifter had his back to her at the moment, but surely he would turn.

The ladies' room; that always worked. But even as she began to rise, she saw that she was too late. The waitress was coming.

Oh, hell, oh, hell, oh, hell, oh, helllll.

She saw *him* turn with lifted brows and a wry smile in his strong angular face as the waitress began her smoking journey. As the waitress kept approaching, she blanked, then desperately dropped her purse from her lap. She ducked after it.

"I'll get it, Serena," Marc murmured.

"No, no," she gasped. It wouldn't take long enough for her to merely retrieve her purse. She hit the clasp with what she prayed was an unobtrusive motion and allowed its contents to spill out. She closed her eyes for a second as she heard the clink of glass upon the table.

But then the waitress was asking if she could help.

"No, really!" Serena called up from the floor brightly. "I just about have everything." She was sure Marc was thinking her crazy now—and wondering why the hell she had picked this particular evening to apparently lose her grace and dignity. But things could be far worse.

"What are you doing down there?" Jerry demanded.

"My, ah, lipstick rolled."

It really had. Serena slipped from her chair to reach far beneath the table. She began to shimmy back out, then noted with horror a pair of boots on the other side of the table. Somehow she knew before she heard the voice.

"Excuse me, but what are those things?"

Jerry Kloon laughed and beckoned the waitress to return with the drink menu. And Serena froze.

Marc dipped his head quickly during the exchange.

"Serena! Would you get off the floor!" he hissed.

He noticed the interchange. "Have you dropped something? Allow me."

She tried to get to her feet, but her heel caught her dress. She was still on the floor as he came around. She was forced to slowly, slowly meet his eyes as he knelt before her.

He didn't say a word; the shock registered in his eyes. She gave him a look of raw horror that mixed once more with the electrical impact of feeling him near once more.

She literally wanted to die.

But some self-preservation instinct suddenly rose to save her. She accepted her lipstick from his frozen, outstretched hand and managed to get to her feet. "Thank you," she mumbled before dashing out an "Excuse me" and finally making good her retreat—a mad dash out of the lounge and into that sanctity of sanctities, the ladies' room.

It was the coward's way out, she chastised herself. She should have had some cool. She should have thought of something to say—she should have managed to pretend she had never seen him before in her life. Right now she should set her chin high and waltz back in to regain her seat with calm and poise.

No way.

She remained in the ladies' room for a good ten minutes. Even for Marc, even for the cause of his book, she couldn't walk back into that lounge. Her mind began ticking; she prayed that the man would retreat with his knowledge of the drink. They were in Boston; he might be staying in that hotel. Maybe there was a weight lifters convention, a Mr. America contest going on. He had only been on a day excursion to Salem; she wouldn't run into him again.

Marc and Jerry would eventually have to leave the lounge.

Marc was probably going to want to kill her.

But so, apparently, did *he,* Joe Jock. She had seen it in his shocked stare. And he was definitely the worst of two evils.

No, no, no, she was not going back in the lounge. Not if the devil rose from hell to drag her in.

She began to wish that she were a practicing witch, that she could cast a spell that would make the ground open beneath *his* feet and swallow him up in a single bite. Or that she could cast a spell that would glue his tongue to the roof of his mouth, make each of those defined muscles of his weigh a ton and drag him halfway through to China.

Oh, God! How had a single day turned her life into a nightmare?

She washed her face with cool water and gritted her teeth as she ventured out into the hallway. Thank God. Jerry and Marc were walking from the lounge toward her. Marc looked puzzled and not a little angry; Jerry Kloon merely looked concerned. Serena looked carefully for anyone behind them, but they were alone. She waved a hand. "Here I am."

She walked toward them with an apology on her lips. "Please, forgive me. I must be coming down with something. The room was beginning to sway on me."

Jerry Kloon interrupted her to assure her that it was he who should apologize; he had made the night a long one. "Go home and get some sleep and take care of yourself. Marc is going to need your help with that 'ghost' novel of his."

Serena swallowed with relief. Marc had gotten the contract.

But Marc hadn't said a word to her. Nor did he as good-byes and thank-yous were exchanged. He didn't speak until they were in his aging Cutlass and on the highway headed home.

Then he exploded. "What the hell were you trying to do to me? You know how desperately I needed this contract! Christ, Serena, it was as if you were going out of your way to make the night a disaster! And we can't all have been lucky enough to have married for money—especially an older spouse kind enough to die quickly—"

"Marc!" The sick horror of his anger-spurred accusation snapped her from all other thoughts, and the exclamation she gave him was a sure sign that he had stepped too far, that his words were unforgivable.

His jaw tightened as he drove; he blinked painfully. "I'm sorry, Serena, I really am. I should never have said that, and believe me, honey, I didn't mean it. It's just that I can't begin to understand you tonight. What is the matter with you?"

Torn between anger and guilt, Serena bit down on her lip with no reply. Marc decided to give her silence meaning.

"It was that story about Eleanora, wasn't it!" he exclaimed exaltedly. "It does bother you. I know, Serena, that you sense things, know things. Don't you see how you could be helping me? If you gave me the slightest bit of assistance, Serena, we could do wonderful things—"

"Marc!" Serena hissed out. "Stop it! I mean it! I don't see things and I don't sense things and I don't want my life or my home turned into absurdities! You caused tonight! You know that I don't believe in ghosts, that I've never heard a thing in the Golden Hawk, and you were trying to get me to lie to that man! I won't do it, Marc—and you've gotten your almighty contract! Leave it be!"

They both fell silent. Serena's aggravation with him was such that she was beginning to wonder why she felt so terribly guilty.

Because in his way Marc had been wonderful; he had been an undemanding companion. He had been there over the last year when she needed him, and yet when she calls a stop to his needs, he laughs and tells her a time will come.

"Oh, Lord," she moaned suddenly, "do I have a headache."

They rode in silence again; then his hand reached out to clutch hers in sympathy. "Serena," he said finally, softly, "I'm sorry. I realize you're tired, I realize I tried to twist your hand. Thank you for tonight, and forgive me."

She bit down so hard on her lip that she tasted blood.

"I'm the sorry one, Marc," she murmured, breathing deeply.

A wave of trembling seemed to sweep over her, and she ground down on her teeth, turning to him and wondering how she was managing to talk and move so deceitfully. But she was doing just that. She smiled as if all were totally clear between them. "By the way," she murmured, "who was that man?"

"What man?" Marc frowned.

"The one who came to the table to ask about the drinks."

"Oh." Marc shrugged. "I don't know. Jerry answered him, but then he left, mumbling a thank-you as if he hadn't even heard."

Breathing suddenly became a lot easier, Serena discovered. She lay back in the seat and closed her eyes, unaware that Marc still held her hand. Minutes later they reached the Golden Hawk.

"You know," Marc murmured as he walked her to the kitchen door, "I should really move in to work on the book. I'll be spending half my time here to begin with—it would be much easier."

"I'd have nowhere to put you," Serena replied. "The three rooms are already rented for the summer. I have my usual two older couples, and Martha rented out the last room for the summer a week ago—to some old professor researching the 'clinical psychology' of the witchcraft trials."

Marc took her key and inserted it in the lock and led her into the kitchen, smiling as he closed the door behind them and pinned her lightly against it. "You know," he whispered huskily close to her face, "you could break down and let me sleep in your room."

She had to laugh; was he teasing or was he serious? They had been through this before; he had often hinted at marriage. And he knew she still didn't feel herself a widow long enough to try it again.

"No answer?" he queried with a long sigh that was dramatic. "Oh, cruel vixen, I'll keep suffering!" He moved even closer for a good night kiss.

It was the strangest kiss she had ever received. Her mind and body swept back stubbornly to that touch of lips at the pond, and suddenly she felt nothing. Not a stirring, not warmth, certainly not passion. And at the same time, a great sadness hit her. She should love Marc. She should want him, but she didn't.

Guilt, and a pain more terrible than ever before, rose within her, and she made herself return the kiss. Feigned passion was better than none. He deserved so much more.

And when he released her, murmuring a soft, "Ummmm," she brought a tremulous smile to her lips. "See you later," he murmured insinuatively, stepping aside, reopening the door, and leaving her with a blown kiss—a charade of a newlywed spouse leaving only to park a car or put out the garbage before returning.

Serena chuckled at his antics, then sobered painfully. What was the matter with her? She had lost her head at the pond, and she was ready to throw a decent relationship away because of it. How stupid. Absurd. She shouldn't have done what she did, but she had. It was over. And she had seen Joe Jock—he was real, too real. He had come after her in the pond, enjoyed a wild interlude, then run off to keep his dinner appointment with another woman!

She had done the same thing.

But I didn't go after him, she excused herself.

Musing, she turned to lock the door, telling herself she should be grateful that nothing further had happened in the lounge.

"I thought you weren't married."

The sound froze her rigidly. Now she was hearing things. This time, it couldn't be, it absolutely couldn't be.

But as she turned slowly, horror restricting her every motion, she began to see things as well as hear them.

It was him, leaning against the shadow of the refrigerator. A scream rose in her throat, but it gave no sound. He straightened and began walking toward her, skirting the heavy oak table that sat in the middle of the room. He was stripped of jacket and tie. His shirt was a pale beige that now opened at the neck to contrast sharply with the dark bronze of his skin and the darkly curled hair that rose in the vee created by the opened buttons.

"You told me you weren't married," he repeated, pausing just before her. Not close enough to touch, but close enough so that she could smell his pleasantly masculine scent, feel the electricity of his body heat that seemed to be generated in lashing waves.

"He's not my husband," she heard herself saying stupidly.

He paused with a very dry grin that was more snarl than smile and a disdainfully mocking brow arched high. "Then my Lord, Mrs. Loren, you do get around."

Serena closed her eyes briefly and swallowed, realizing he thought she did jump from bed to bed adulterously. What the hell did she care what he thought? They should never have met; he didn't own her—what a thought—he appeared to think absolutely nothing of their interlude. And how dare he condemn her when she had seen him with . . .

A shaft of jealousy whipped through her, which made her more furious than she had been to begin with. "You're trespassing again," she said hotly. "I don't know who you are or what the hell you think you're doing, but this time I want you off my property—before I call the police."

His second brow joined the first in a high arch, and with his grin becoming exasperatingly pleasant, he crossed his massive arms over his muscled chest. "Do you call the police on all your guests, Mrs. Loren? Is that part of the inn's particular brand of hospitality."

"Guests," Serena repeated blankly. She shook her head disbelievingly. "I have no rooms," she murmured, wondering how he had gotten into the kitchen to begin with. "My last was just rented," she continued to stutter, praying suddenly that she hadn't become involved with a dangerous lunatic. "Really. I haven't got a room in the place. There are only three. I have two elderly couples who come every summer, and, and . . . a college professor. Dr. . . . umm . . . O'Neill. Really. You can look at the register."

He was laughing at her. Dear God, he was a lunatic. And he was taking a step closer. He reached to touch her chin, and she could do nothing but freeze.

"My lovely Mrs. Loren, please don't look so worried. I am Dr. O'Neill." He stepped away from her, with something that was very dark and dangerous in his tumultuous hazel eyes. He turned to walk for the hallway door with a brisk step, then paused, spun on a heel, and faced her once more.

"It was truly a pleasure to meet you, Mrs. Loren. Truly a pleasure."

With a slight salute he smiled that deathly pleasant smile and left her.

CHAPTER THREE

She had endured a truly rotten night. Finding Marc at her front door hauling a large package at seven thirty A.M. did little to improve her mood.

"What on earth are you doing?" Serena demanded, her tone hinting at her irritation as he pushed through the open door with his prize. "Marc, I have to get ready for work—"

"I know, I know, Serena," Marc replied with enthusiasm underlying his impatience. "But I found *this* just half an hour ago, and I had to show it to you."

Serena stood back with a frown as Marc dragged his slim, three-by-four-foot brown, wrapped package into the hallway and began to tear away at the paper. "I was passing Mrs. Lund's flea market in Danvers, and I saw it—you know how early she sets up—and I practically drove off the road. Not that I knew what it was at first, but, well . . . just a second here, and you'll see what I mean! Voilà!"

The paper fell away, and Serena gasped. It was an old painting—faded and chipped, but pricelessly old. Yet what held her in stunned amazement was not the obvious historical value of the piece, but its subject. The woman who stared from the canvas with a soft smile on her lips belying sad, knowing eyes was uncannily familiar. Serena stared at a very similar face each morning as she put on her makeup.

"Told you!" Marc said smugly.

Serena bent for a more thorough scrutiny of the painting. The woman was clad in a gray wool dress highlighted only by a large white collar in typical Puritan conservatism. She sat upon a stiff-backed chair, her hands folded demurely in her lap. Her hair was dark; it was drawn back from her face severely, but a few wisps of curling ebony escaped that severity with an undeniable defiance to softly frame her face.

Serena couldn't possibly pretend to deny that the face was like her own. Although the colors of the oils utilized by the artist were fading, it was apparent that the woman was intended to have blue eyes—deeply blue, dark to a point of violet. The cheekbones were slimmer than Serena's, the chin sharper; the nose lacked the little insolent tilt of Serena's, but still, despite the drastic difference in hair shade, the woman in the picture and Serena bore a startling resemblance.

"Well, Eleanora, what do you say?" Marc teased.

Serena glanced at him sharply. "How do you know this is Eleanora?"

"Oh, Serena! You disappoint me!" Marc said, clicking his tongue. "Look closely at the hands."

Serena peered closely at the canvas once more. One of the elegantly folded fingers bore a ring, and as Serena narrowed her eyes, she realized that the ring was formed of a delicately carved *E*.

Serena sat back on her heels and glanced at Marc. "It's something, all right," she murmured. "I can't believe it's appeared now, after all these centuries—if it's authentic, that is. Where did Mrs. Lund say she got it?"

Marc laughed. "She's had it for years and years, but didn't know it—it was painted over. Her nephew is an art student—he told her about a month ago that he believed that there was a painting beneath the seascape she thought she had. They were both quite excited—Mrs. Lund thought she might be harboring a masterpiece. She was quite disappointed to discover she wasn't holding a Raphael or the like. Eleanora's artist was an unknown, I'm afraid. It's rather surprising that the portrait was painted at all at that time!"

Serena nodded vaguely and shrugged. "I would have it authenticated anyway, if I were you. Not," she added dryly, "that I think you paid Mrs. Lund an exorbitant sum."

"Fifty bucks!" Marc laughed.

"Marc," Serena complained, "that's highway robbery! How could you do that to the poor woman?"

"Poor woman! She's loaded! And I'm a struggling author—"

"That's not the point—"

"And you're missing the point! Serena, that *is* you! Aren't you feeling tingles?"

Serena sighed with clenched teeth. "Marc—I don't know what you're getting at, but that isn't me. I grant you the resemblance is startling, but don't go getting on one of your kicks. If anything—" She broke off as the doorbell began to ring.

"I'll get it," Marc murmured dourly.

From her crouched position in the hallway, Serena watched as Marc opened the door.

To her horror she saw that it was the guest who had first disrupted her entire life, then added insult to injury by stealing even her sleep with the audacity of being in her house.

He had apparently been jogging. A leather band held slick wet hair from his brow, and he was clad in a pair of loose shorts and a tank top. Little of his astounding physique was left to the imagination, and yet he was a man apparently unaware of his remarkable assets. He was leaning against the doorframe breathing heavily, his bronze skin glistening with a sheen of perspiration as Marc opened the door.

Serena felt her own breath catch; the picture had erased him from her mind for a heaven-sent interlude, but now a wave of new horror and humiliation washed over her like an entire ocean. She had spent part of her sleepless night wondering how she would deal with him when she saw him again, and how she would deal with his inevitable meeting with Marc. But surely Marc would recognize him only as the stranger in the restaurant, and he *was* a stranger. Surely a stranger wouldn't say anything in front of Marc, especially when that stranger was apparently well versed in one-night affairs.

In those few seconds her mind spun so quickly it was almost as if everything that happened did so in slow motion.

Marc didn't even recognize him as the stranger in the restaurant. He took one look at the he-man build and started to absently close the door with a casual, "Deliveries to the rear, please."

A hand came out to stop the door from closing. "Excuse me —I'm not delivering anything."

Serena would have laughed at the noticeable irritation in the painfully civil protest except that she was feeling pathetically unnerved. Her blood had seemed to heat at the sound of his voice; her hands became instantly clammy. She had to concentrate merely to stand, and then, once she was on her feet, she found herself plunging in and nervously chattering at a frantic pace.

"Marc, this is, uh, Dr. O'Neill. He's taken the third guest room for the summer. Dr. O'Neill, I'd like you to meet a friend of mine, Marc Talbot. Dr. O'Neill is a—" For the life of her, Serena couldn't remember exactly what Martha had said the "old Doc" did. "He's a—"

"Psychologist," Justin O'Neill offered dryly. "Clinical psychologist."

The two men shook hands somewhat warily. Serena was aware that Marc's reaction to O'Neill was not dissimilar to her own. The man had no right being any type of an intellectual. He should have been driving a semi-truck, or wielding a hockey stick—or fighting off lions with his bare hands in a Roman arena.

"Sorry to have interrupted you," O'Neill apologized with a sarcasm only Serena seemed to notice. "I forgot to take the main door key with me." He released Marc's hand, and his piercing hazel eyes with their sardonic depths turned to Serena.

"You weren't really interrupting anything, Dr. O'Neill," Serena returned with what she hoped was a cool nonchalance.

She kept wondering how Marc didn't sense the tension in the small hallway, tension that was so thick it might be cut with a knife.

But Marc didn't seem to think anything. After a moment he appeared to accept the psychologist/jogger with little thought. His appearance, in fact, seemed providential.

"A clinical psychologist, eh?" Marc queried, and Serena winced inwardly, as she knew what was coming by his self-satisfied tone. "A man of science—just whom I'd like to see at the moment." He beckoned to Justin O'Neill to come around to see the painting. "Take a look at the picture, and then take a good look at our Mrs. Loren. What do you say?"

O'Neill stared at the picture for a long time. Then he turned his fathomless gaze back to Serena. "I say it's a bit of a resemblance," he remarked, then shrugged. "An extraordinary resemblance, Mrs. Loren."

"Extraordinary," he said, but not "uncanny." Despite the fact that she still wished the man might disappear into a hole in the earth, she was suddenly grateful for his tone. Yes, it was extraordinary—but interestingly so, nothing else.

She didn't know she had been holding her breath until she expelled a long sigh. Then she closed her eyes momentarily. She was in the middle of an "extraordinary" turmoil, trying to control the shiver that had come over her since he had come near, but if she didn't get herself together, she was going to be up an "extraordinary" creek; the chamber of commerce would be revoking their endorsement if she didn't get her business opened on schedule this morning in the height of the summer tourist season.

"Well," she murmured, lowering her eyes from both men, "if you'll excuse me, I want to get some breakfast and get out of here."

"Think Martha will feed me?" Marc inquired hopefully.

"She never refuses you," Serena said dryly, biting her lip as she realized she had just informed her intimate stranger that this other man was a frequent guest. What difference did it

57

make? She didn't even know if he had realized yet that she wasn't an adulteress.

What do I care what he thinks? her mind shrieked. He seduced me and disappeared and then had the utter gall to reappear.

The stranger passed her with his infuriating smile, and she dimly realized that he had excused himself to shower for breakfast. She had to blink to come back to life once more, and coming back to life was misery. She was so physically aware of him again as he brushed her, aware of his very masculine scent, aware of the glistening bronze muscles.

He didn't get them just from jogging, she thought resentfully. How had a city college professor become so darkly tanned, so incredibly sinewed? It wasn't fair.

"Serena, I swear I don't know what is wrong with you lately. You're continually off in some kind of dream—"

"Oh, sorry, Marc," Serena murmured, whirling around quickly. "Come on, let's go to the dining room." Once more she was moving like a whippet, having realized that if she hurried, she could be out of the dining room before Dr. O'Neill reappeared.

"Wait a minute," Marc said. "Just let me set the painting before the wall."

Serena left Marc adjusting his portrait and hurried into the kitchen. It was exactly eight, and Martha was piling a plate high with blueberry biscuits. "Take these, will you, dear?" Martha told Serena, handing her the plate without bothering to wait for a reply. "The Bakers and the Donnesys aren't having breakfast this morning," Martha told Serena, her brown eyes sparkling as she smoothed back neat gray curls before reaching for the massive coffeepot. "They all left at the crack of dawn to go whale watching."

Serena laughed, the sparkle in her eyes matching that of Martha's affectionately. The Donnesys and the Bakers were all four on the far side of seventy, but more active, life-loving people she had yet to meet. She had looked forward to their coming for the summer leaving their southern retreats to stay at the inn.

"Good for them!" Serena said, but then her smile faded as she followed Martha from the kitchen to the elegantly cared for dining room. Only one of three tables had been set—Martha had planned for Dr. O'Neill to join them.

"I heard Marc's voice," Martha said with a shade of exasperation. She wasn't terribly fond of the number of meals she afforded the young man. "So I assumed he was staying." The prim note left her voice. "Wait until you meet Dr. O'Neill! You're really going to enjoy him, Serena! Not that he's a thing like I expected—I mean a professor?—but you'll see! He's doing a book up here, you know. Kind of a heavy thing, I take it. He's totally against the witchcraft trials being presented historically as cases of fraud and the like—he was trying to explain to me how very terrible and physical the clinical type of hysteria could be! And he can tell you all sorts of fascinating things! He's studied voodoo and African arts and Indian shamans and —but he's not at all the bookish type. Like I said, just wait till you see him, dear—my Lord, I do run on."

She certainly had run on. Serena hadn't been able to find a second in which to interrupt. "Martha," she murmured, following the older woman back into the kitchen to be handed a large platter of bacon, "I've met Dr. O'Neill."

"Oh!" Martha paused and scrutinized Serena sharply. "Well?"

"Well what?"

"What did you think?"

Serena lowered her eyes. I wasn't actually thinking when we first met, she thought bitterly. She shrugged, turning with her bacon. "He seems all right," she said nonchalantly.

"Did I hear you say something about a book?"

Marc entered the dining room and pulled out a chair for himself.

"Yes," Martha said, her eyes narrowing upon her unwanted guest. "Dr. O'Neill writes textbooks that are used in colleges and universities all over the country."

"Who told you that?" Marc inquired a bit sourly. "Dr. O'Neill?"

59

Martha gave him a thin-lipped smile. "No, Marc. When he called to reserve the room, he mentioned he was writing a book. I happened to mention him to Mrs. Baker. *She* told me that he was considered the best in his field!"

Serena hated to hear the sharp edge passing between two of her best friends. But there was no help for it. Martha and Marc simply didn't get along, and although open warfare had never been declared, situations had been known to get tense. She took the seat beside Marc and lied valiantly with false cheer. "It should be an exciting summer—a clinical writer and an imaginative one—both haunting the Golden Hawk!"

Just as she finished speaking, the "clinical" writer made his appearance. Bathed and shaved, and both casual and overwhelmingly vigorous in jeans and a sport shirt, he offered a pleasant "Good morning" to Martha before taking the chair beside Serena.

"I hear you're a writer," Marc said to him. Serena heard the defensive quality to his tone and winced. You aren't in competition, Marc, she thought sadly, except it was easy to understand his feelings. As she had noted herself, the doctor was a bit of an awesome shock. A power like nothing she had ever known. It was only natural that he had Marc off base. First he had discovered that he was venturing into his first big novel along parallel lines with an acclaimed veteran. To second that affront, the acclaimed veteran towered over his medium height, and besides being brilliant, Justin had also managed to become an astounding physical specimen.

And, oh God, Marc, Serena thought a little sickly, he's also another one up on you.

She couldn't seem to control the color from flooding her face with thought of her own capitulation to the good doctor. She lowered her head and pretended an engrossed concentration upon buttering a muffin.

Justin O'Neill shrugged in reply to Marc. "I'm a teacher," he said, "who writes on the side. Nothing terribly exciting most of the time, I'm afraid. Especially to the grad students studying for their exams."

Martha and Marc chuckled at the dry comment; Serena felt her muffin catch in her throat. A shiver caught hold of her, and she picked up her coffee cup, wincing as the hot liquid burned in her throat. Suddenly she could stand the absurdity of the situation no longer. She stood and murmured, "You'll all have to excuse me. I want to get to work."

Marc glanced at her strangely; Justin O'Neill rose. "I look forward to seeing you later, Mrs. Loren. Martha has informed me that you're a wealth of information—and I'd very much like to hear the history of the inn . . . from you."

There was the slightest pause between the words, but to Serena their implication was deep.

"I'd be willing to help you all I can," Marc offered. "If you're after intriguing history, that would be Eleanora Hawk—the woman in the portrait we showed you this morning."

"I've heard the story," O'Neill mused in reply to Marc, his eyes still on Serena. "The resemblance becomes all the more interesting though. Do you think there is an explanation, Mrs. Loren?"

Marc started to speak, but Serena, aware of the mystic meaning he would give, quickly interrupted.

"Certainly there's a plausible, clinical explanation, Dr. O'Neill. I'm a widow, and therefore, a Loren. But my maiden name was Hawk. Long range genetics, but genetics nevertheless. Now, if you will please excuse me . . ."

She fled the room before anyone could say anything else. When she reached her car, she was shaking. She gripped the wheel tightly for a moment and took a deep breath. What a fool she was being. The man was making her a nervous wreck. And on top of it all, Marc was becoming convinced she was a reincarnation of a long-dead ancestor.

"And everything was going so well," she murmured aloud to herself in bewilderment. Impatiently she twisted her key in the ignition and drove down the long sloping drive to the highway.

The Museum of Fact and Fantasy was located in the center of town. As a child she had dreamed of opening such a place, and when she had married Bill Loren, she had laughingly told him her dream. "Silly dream, I guess," she had said. "Salem is already full of attractions."

"The only silly dream," her husband had replied, "is one that you don't attempt to accomplish."

Serena bit her lip with her thoughts. She had loved Bill Loren dearly, with all her heart. He had been twenty years her senior, but it hadn't mattered to either of them.

She bit into her lip harder. It had been a long time since she had cried. He had been dead two years. She had spent the first year learning to live without him, nursing her memories with tears at night. And then, when she had realized she couldn't mourn forever, she had been afraid. Her friends had dated, and frequently they had affairs with married men who were unfaithful, men who were either chauvinistic, or totally dependent. Two of her close friends were divorced after disastrous marriages: Karen's husband hadn't been able to make a decision between her and an old lover; Beth's husband had left her when her income as an artist had surpassed his as an accountant.

Bill had been the perfect mate. Strong and secure, he could both love and trust her. He cheered on each of her triumphs, held her hand and promised the sun would rise during disasters.

Martha, strangely enough, had been the one to finally talk her into dating Marc. He had come to Salem from Boston to work for the local newspaper, and he had apparently become determined to date Serena from the first day he saw her at the museum. She had eventually given in to his persistence. And she had slowly learned that going out could be fun.

Serena wondered suddenly if she had discovered that life could not only be fun, but comfortable. Being with Marc was easy. She knew his insecurities, and if she sometimes found them annoying, she would shrug and remind herself that no one was perfect.

What is the matter with me, she wondered? I'm suddenly finding fault with Marc because . . . because of that stinking Dr. O'Neill, she thought irritably. All because of a case of temporary insanity!

She groaned aloud with the thought that her temporary insanity had turned her existence into madness. How was she going to deal with the man in her house all summer?

"Worry about it later!" she muttered aloud as she unlocked the doors to the museum and flicked on the light switch. A large, horned devil glared at her from the wall of the entryway, and she glared back. "I feel worse than you look!" she told the stained-glass caricature.

"And you *do* look like hell!"

Serena turned with a dry grimace for her assistant, Susan Aspach. "Thanks. I love to begin the day with flattery."

Nonplussed, Susan laughed and plopped her huge macrame bag over the ticket counter. She was a pretty, pixyish blonde with deep brown eyes and a happy-go-lucky manner that never failed.

She was also a practicing "white witch."

"What's the matter?" she inquired, raising a brow to Serena. "Things go wrong with Marc's publisher? Marc looked in high enough spirits himself."

Serena frowned. "You saw Marc?"

"Yeah." Susan leaned over the counter to check for a roll of tickets, then brushed past Serena to open the secondary doors and illuminate the displays in appropriate mist-blue fluorescences. "I stopped by the inn," she called over her shoulder, heels clicking across the stone floor of the main room as she headed for the rear of the building which housed the small book and gift shop and tiny office.

Following in the wake of her hyper friend, Serena demanded, "Why?"

"What?" Susan was already pouring water through the Mr. Coffee machine. "Oh—I don't know. I had just thought we might ride in together, but I missed you."

"Oh," Serena murmured.

"Well?"

"What?"

Susan shook her head and laughed. "Gee, maybe we'd better start all over this morning! My 'well?' meant what's wrong? Did the dinner go badly?"

63

Serena shook her head. "No, the dinner didn't go badly. It went well. Marc is going to get his advance. I didn't get much sleep last night."

Susan lifted a brow but queried her no further. She had her own answer. "It's the painting," she said, nodding sagely.

"You saw the painting?"

"Umm—Marc showed it to me. It gave me shivers, Serena."

"Oh, stop!" Serena wailed.

"You're going to try and tell me there isn't a resemblance?"

Serena sighed, counting slowly to ten. "Yes, there's a resemblance—but it isn't that shocking."

Susan shrugged. "Coffee?"

"Yes, I could use the whole pot."

She accepted a cup of coffee from Susan and idly ran her fingers over the invoices she had left on the desk the night before. Susan sipped her coffee with a long sigh.

"What did you think of Dr. O'Neill?" Serena asked, trying to keep the question casual.

"Who?"

"My summer guest," Serena explained.

"Oh, I didn't meet him. What's he like?"

When directly asked the question, Serena wasn't sure what to say. She answered slowly. "I don't know . . . strange for a professor. He's much younger than I expected. And he jogs and looks like he should be surfing or weight lifting. Muscle-bound type."

"Bad vibes."

"What?" Serena said, feeling ridiculous. She was accustomed to having strange conversations with Susan, but this morning she felt as if they were in different dimensions.

"You have bad vibes about him—or maybe it's the picture," Susan said solemnly.

"I don't have bad vibes about anything!" Serena groaned with exasperation. "I just had a bad night!"

Susan shrugged with a knowing look, and Serena wanted to shake her. Sometimes having a practicing witch for a friend and employee was extremely trying. She turned for the office door with her coffee cup. "I'm going out front—I think it's opening time."

"Hey!" Susan protested. "I'm tickets today. It's your turn to be the guide into the occult!"

Serena grimaced. It *was* her turn.

"Don't you want to switch?" she asked hopefully.

"Nope," Susan said, shaking her head firmly.

Serena shrugged. The museum was hers, and she was the boss, but she and Susan had always worked as equals—which was the only way Serena could see it, since she wouldn't have been able to manage the place without Susan.

Serena made a face but reached for the black cloak and pointed hat that hung on the rack beside the door.

"This really doesn't seem fair," she grumbled good-naturedly, "since you're the one who *is* a witch!"

Susan raised her coffee cup. "We'll welcome you into the coven anytime!" She laughed.

Serena replied with a dry look and walked back into the main sector of the building. The displays, which were composed of beautifully crafted wax figures, were in three segments: Magic Through the Ages, Witchcraft in Salem in 1692, and the Different Faces of Witchcraft. Each tabloid had a stereo recording, but visitors entered in groups on the half hour and were first greeted by either herself or Susan. They were given a brief explanation of the difference between "white" and "black" magic and of several tools of the craft which had remained constant through the centuries. Then the "witch" guide would retire to the gift shop.

Susan swept on by Serena with a smile. "Which witch is which?" she purred sweetly.

"Droll, Susan, very droll," Serena called after her. She adjusted the sweeping black cloak and her pointed hat. As she waited for the tour to begin, she slipped behind the distance fence to check the wax figures. She chewed upon her lip as she studied the panorama of Satan in his goat form surrounded by three witches and their familiars.

The goat Satan was beginning to lose some of his hair. She sighed. Several of her figures needed face-lifts.

A tap on the door warned her that the first group of the day was ready. Serena swung open the double doors and smiled, and then went into her introduction of the pentagon and the circle of power.

The day seemed endless to her. She and Susan were only able to slip away for a half hour lunch break, and when they returned, people awaited them in a line on the sidewalk.

"Summer," Susan muttered.

"Umm," Serena agreed. She should be glad of the business; the overhead for keeping the museum afloat was high, and as she had noted earlier, some of the figures needed repair. And she wanted to add some new exhibits. Her enthusiasm was usually high—the museum was, after all, her creation.

But besides being tired, she was a nervous wreck. Her mind kept hopping from the incredible incident at the pond to the disastrous dinner, to the miserable fact that Marc and the overwhelming Dr. O'Neill would both be hovering about her home all summer.

"I wish I knew a spell to make people drop through sidewalks," Susan murmured as they were forced to excuse their way through the waiting crowd to open the door.

"Susan!" Serena chuckled. "Such a malicious thought shouldn't come to a nice white witch! But if you do figure out how to manage such a thing, be sure to teach me!"

With the last tour group of the day browsing through the gift shop, Serena excused herself from a group of college students and hurried back into the museum to switch out the fluorescent lights. She was long accustomed to her wax figures, but for some reason she felt goose bumps rise on her arms as she passed by the display case with the stereotype witch—an old hag with a warty nose stirring a potion in her cauldron. Serena shook herself lightly and reached for the switch—

And felt a hand descend over her cloak-clad shoulder.

She stifled back a scream and spun around wide-eyed. When

66

she met the sardonic and querying gaze of Justin O'Neill, she began to wish that a demon had arisen from hell to accost her.

There probably wouldn't be much difference. His eyes definitely held the burning light of the devil.

"Lovely cape," he murmured. "But I do hope you're wearing something beneath it today."

Serena wrenched her shoulder from his touch furiously. "What are you doing here?" she hissed.

His brows lifted in polite inquiry. "The establishment is open to the public, isn't it?"

Serena stared into his eyes for a second, then flicked out the lights and brushed past him, calling over her shoulder, "The establishment is closing for the evening."

"That's exactly why I'm here now."

The strong but low-keyed timbre of his voice brought her to a halt with her back to him.

"Don't you think it might be a nice idea to talk—alone? Or would you prefer to spend your days hopping about like a nervous bird every time I walk into a room?"

Serena turned slowly. In the darkness she could see but a silhouette of him, towering as he stood with arms crossed.

"We, ah, we really don't have anything to talk about," Serena murmured nervously. "A quirk of fate left us both in rather uncomfortable positions—"

His quick, throaty laughter broke off her words. "A quirk of fate? My, my, Mrs. Loren, what happened to all the romance and passion in your soul?"

Serena bit her lip and blushed furiously, thankful then that they stood without light.

"Dr. O'Neill—"

"My name is Justin. Pardon the familiarity, but I really do feel ridiculous being addressed formally by *you.*"

Serena caught a breath and held it, counting. "All right, Justin, I'll admit you make me as nervous as a cat. So we'll talk—quickly. Whatever happened—happened. But it obviously has nothing to do with our day-to-day lives—"

"Oh, on the contrary . . ." he interrupted, beginning a

stealthy walk toward her that made Serena edge backwards. "Considering our daily lives at the present, our encounter certainly affects them!"

He had paused just before her. He didn't touch her, but she could feel him, and it was the same drugging sensation she had felt before. When he was near, she felt compelled to touch him. The scent of him . . . the aura . . . whatever . . . was a lure she had never experienced before. She didn't know him at all, but she felt as if she had known him for ages. Right then and there, she could have dropped all thoughts of anything around them, time, place, people, and move into his arms, and it would have been right.

Serena closed her eyes and struggled with the absurdity of her thoughts. He might be a professor and not the brainless mass of muscles she had assumed him, but he was still some kind of a jock with a startling and overwhelming masculinity who could seduce a woman in the woods and then leave her to rush to a dinner date with another woman.

She opened her mouth to speak, not caring that he saw her back away from him warily again. "Listen, Dr. O'Neill—Justin, I think that there just really isn't a point—"

"There is a point," he corrected, following her. Serena really didn't want to bring her little discussion to the attention of the patrons still loitering in the gift shop, so her continual sidestepping began to take her back through the dark museum.

"I really want some answers," he said flatly.

Serena backed straight into the arms of a horned fertility god and almost fell over. Justin stretched out his arms and steadied her, laughing.

"Dinner?" he inquired.

"What?"

"Dinner. The meal one eats when it's evening."

Serena stared blankly at the cotton-clad arm that steadied her, feeling the tension and heat of the man.

"I, I can't. I mean, you don't understand. I have obligations—" she murmured in a whisper.

"No, no obligations, and no trouble," he persisted. In the

68

darkness the low huskiness of his voice was as smooth as velvet but as firm as steel. "I've told Martha that I intended to try and corner you alone. And your—friend Mr. Talbot has driven to the historical society in Boston to have his painting authenticated. Forget the excuses, witch"—he paused to pull the pointed cap from her head—"because I mean to have a long, long talk with you."

Once again Serena closed her eyes and prayed silently for a strength to come to her so that she might break the spell he cast upon her. She opened her eyes and pulled from his grasp.

"All right, O'Neill," she said irritably. "We'll go to dinner!" She stooped to retrieve the hat that had fallen to the floor and walked briskly for the rear door. "I have to close the register and lock up for the night. If you'll wait out front, I'm sure Susan will entertain you. You just might find her very interesting, Professor. Susan is a real witch. But then you don't believe in magic, do you?"

She wasn't quite sure if his laughter was bitter or amused.

"I don't believe in magic, Mrs. Loren, but I certainly do believe in witchcraft. . . ."

CHAPTER FOUR

He was perfectly polite and casual as they drove, commenting on the landscape. He wasn't awkward with his speech, nor did he chatter—he simply seemed comfortable.

On the other hand, Serena felt as if she were wired, a time bomb ready to explode. From the corner of an eye she watched him, thinking it strange that he could look so nice in the light cotton jacket, so trim and sleek. So civil. Unclothed, he didn't look at all civil.

She dropped her eyes to her lap at the thought, her mind seeming to screech—and she was back to the main question.

How could she have ever done such a thing?

"I must compliment you on the museum," he said casually, glancing her way and returning his vision to the road. "You do a marvelous job defining the difference between facts and fantasy."

"Thank you," Serena said stiffly.

"Not at all."

He fell silent after his reply, and Serena found her own curiosity blooming despite her discomfort.

"What type of book are you doing?" she inquired. "Another thing on the fraud and hysteria that created the trials?"

He grinned dryly. "Nope. I'm going to try to vindicate the judges and jury."

Startled, Serena momentarily forgot that she was in a miserable position. She twisted in the sports car's bucket seat to watch him. "Really? I don't get it—you don't believe in magic . . ."

"I don't," he told her. "But the majority of the people living during the seventeenth century did. And back then—just like now—there were people practicing witchcraft. Bridget Bishop, the first woman to be hanged in Salem, was definitely fooling around with the black arts. Of course, a lot of innocent people suffered. I doubt if more than four of those who lost their lives ever dabbled in the occult, and out of the hundreds who went to jail, there still probably weren't more than a dozen who were actually witches." He glanced her way with a smile again. "That's where the hysteria comes in. Power of suggestion and all that. I plan to look into several theories that might explain the fits and illnesses of the accused girls. Comparisons with mental patients of the French psychologist Charcot and other doctors of later years. I want to explore the possibility of food poisoning—don't laugh, there is a bacteria that grows on wheat that can give one delusions similar to an LSD trip."

Serena did laugh, but surprisingly with pleasure. "I'm *not* laughing at your theory," she explained quickly. "I'm laughing because I love the sound of the book! It sounds fascinating. Oh, I always feel so sorry for the people who were falsely accused and executed, but I just hate to read all these things where the authors peg the Puritan preacher Cotton Mather as a raving maniac on a crusade. From studying the trial documents, you can see that the leaders tried to be very careful. . . ."

Her voice died away suddenly, and she blushed, turning from him to glance out the window. She hadn't imagined she could possibly find herself speaking to him with such enthusiasm.

Serena cleared her throat and started speaking again with cool and polite formality.

"So you're not into purging Puritans and you don't believe in magic but you do believe in the practice of witchcraft. I assume

71

you don't believe in haunts or spooks. Why are you staying at the Golden Hawk?"

"Oh," he replied vaguely, "even 'clinical' writers like a bit of atmosphere."

He pulled off the road as he spoke and parked in front of a freshly painted, white colonial house. Dim light gleamed from the open windows, and the sounds of clinking silver and mellow chatter could be heard along with soft piano music.

"Ever been here?" he inquired.

Serena shook her head. She hadn't thought to ask where they were going; she had been too concerned about what would be said. And now she realized she hadn't even noticed they had driven north of Salem and Danvers.

"Neither have I," Justin said with a grin and a shrug. "I met my fellow roomers when they returned from their whale-watching trip, and the silver-haired lady—Mrs. Donnesy?" At Serena's nod he continued, "Mrs. Donnesy assured me they make the best New England clam chowder in New England."

Once more Serena found herself chuckling, and then choking on her chuckle as he swung from his seat, slammed his door, and strode around to take her arm as she exited from the car. Just twenty-four hours ago they had met and become instant lovers. And then instant enemies.

And now they seemed to be on some type of an awkward date. Well, maybe he wasn't feeling awkward, but she was still ready to die.

Half the time, at least. . . .

They were seated at a quiet corner table. Justin lifted his brow slightly as she ordered a double manhattan, the corners of his lips twisting as he repeated her preference to the waiter. It was apparent to them both that she needed a stiff drink.

When the waiter left, Justin watched her silently across the table. Serena stared back, studying the planes of his face. His features were very hard, she thought, and yet pleasantly assembled. His nose was very sharp, yet looked appropriate, set between the deep widespread eyes. His was a no-nonsense face, ruggedly uncompromising, but shiveringly compelling. His eyes were both keen and fathomless as he returned her scrutiny, and she almost smiled with the thought that one had only to look at him to realize he was as sharp as a whip. How could she have ever tried to tell herself that he was nothing more than macho muscle? It shouldn't have been at all surprising to learn that he was Dr. O'Neill.

Their drinks were set before them. Justin O'Neill saluted her with a mockingly raised brow.

Serena downed half her glass with the first sip.

"Ummm," he murmured elusively, adding, "You certainly are nervous, aren't you, Mrs. Loren."

Serena shrugged.

"Nervous and quiet," he said dryly. "Okay, I'll start. I had begun to think you were really playing musical beds, but I do realize now that you're a widow. So tell me now about Marc."

Serena had taken another nervous sip at her drink, which now choked her. What on earth was he trying to get at?

She gasped for air and swallowed several times as he watched her with his barely discernible, knowing grin. "Tell you what about Marc?" she snapped. "You've met him. He's a writer. He's thirty-three, five eleven, I believe, and about—"

"Spare me the statistics," Justin interrupted her, his eyes intense now and his smile gone. "I want to know about your relationship."

Serena would have loved to kick herself for the flood of brilliant crimson that heated her face. How could she allow him to affect her this way? "I will not!" she declared firmly. "My relationships are none of your business!"

"They certainly are—you owe me an explanation."

"I owe you!" She almost shrieked the words, then closed her eyes and bit her lip as she noticed she had attracted several pairs of curious eyes to their table. She lowered her voice and hissed, "I don't owe you a thing."

"Have you decided?" he inquired politely.

"On what?"

"Dinner. Remember, it's the meal one eats at night. That's

why we're sitting in a restaurant. That card you're holding is a menu, and from it, you pick what you'd like—"

"Thank you, Professor," Serena interrupted sarcastically. "I know this is a menu, but I really don't care what I eat. Dinner was your idea, and I'm really not terribly hungry."

"Yes," he said quietly, glancing at his menu, "you do owe me an explanation." He glanced back up at her. "Mrs. Donnesy suggested the prime rib."

"Fine."

His brows lifted. "Well?"

Serena shook her head in confusion. "Well what?"

"The explanation."

She was starting to shriek with frustration again. "I don't owe you a thing!" In her effort to quietly but vehemently make her point, she leaned far over the table. "You accosted me on my own property and disappeared, and now—"

"Accosted?" His protest was voiced with mocking irritation.

"All right—seduced!" Serena snapped, her whisper lost to aggravation. Justin lowered his head with a grin, and Serena realized that she once more had the attention of the neighboring tables.

"Oh, God," she moaned softly. "Don't you realize you are embarrassing me terribly?" she demanded.

"A little embarrassment is going to be worth getting a few things straight," Justin replied pragmatically.

The waiter appeared before she could reply. Justin ordered the prime rib for them both. When the waiter had disappeared, Serena clenched her hands beneath the table and forced herself to speak softly and calmly. "Dr. O'Neill, you seduced me and left me so you could rush off to another dinner engagement. That's fine—that's your business—"

"Objection!" He leaned across the table, and she shivered slightly as she came in such close contact with his eyes. "I'm sure you're the one who seduced me."

"The hell I did! I was going swimming—"

"Do you often do things like that?"

"Of course not."

74

He lowered his lashes with a half smile curling his lip. "What was it then, Mrs. Loren, magic?"

Serena was saved by the arrival of their salads. She moved her lettuce around with her fork, started to speak, paused, and began again. "Dr. O'Neill, don't you see how pointless this all is—"

"No, I don't. For one, I didn't leave you. I tried to get a flashlight so that we could talk, and I returned to discover that you'd vanished."

"And then you must have cried all night," Serena observed dryly. "Or for all of two minutes, at least. It didn't take you long to assuage your pain with the lady in Boston."

"You're trying to hang me for that?" Justin demanded with a laugh, almost choking on a cucumber. "You made it to Boston —assuaging your pain—with greater speed than I did."

Serena set her fork down. He was right. They had both had commitments; they had both met them. Neither had planned on the extraordinary meeting at the pond.

She nibbled her lip for a moment with her eyes shielded by the fringe of her lashes, then murmured, "I still don't see where this 'talk' is taking us. Justin, you just made a marvelous point. We both had to be in Boston for dinner commitments."

"I don't think you're getting the point at all this evening," he said slowly. "I want to know just what your commitment is." He watched her as he gave up all pretense of interest in his salad and sipped the dark rum, anejo, with lime. The piercing quality in his eyes made her shiver slightly, and she remembered that from the very first she had thought he would be a man who demanded all.

Serena pushed her own salad aside and drew a ring around the rim of her glass with her forefinger. "Perhaps, Dr. O'Neill, you might like to start with an explanation of your own commitments."

"Certainly," he replied without a blink. "I have none."

"None?" Serena raised a skeptical brow. "You'll excuse me," she added dryly, "for noticing that you seemed well acquainted with the brunette in Boston."

75

"I am well acquainted," he said levelly. "But I am not committed." His hand came across the table, broad and yet tapered. Serena found herself staring at his neatly clipped nails as his fingers arrested the movement of hers over the glass rim.

"Your turn," he informed her grimly.

"I—"

"Are you engaged?"

"No. I—"

"Are you sleeping with him?"

Serena wrenched her fingers from his, furious to feel the heat he could so easily stir fanning across her cheeks. "How dare you ask me a question like that! You're crazy if you think an absurd meeting in the woods gives you any right—"

She broke off, further irritated to see he was shielding his eyes from her with lowered lashes, and that he was apparently attempting to hide the grin that was tugging at his full lips.

"What the hell is so damned amusing?" she demanded.

His eyes rose to hers, and he said quietly, "I'm glad you're not sleeping with him."

"Dammit!" Serena grated out, feeling the hot blush pervade her body from head to toe. Her fingers wound tightly around her glass, and she glared at him with her eyes blazing the wrath which was compounded by the terrible effect he had upon her. "I certainly didn't say that I wasn't—"

"You didn't have to say anything," he interrupted coolly.

"Your ego must be the size of your biceps," Serena snapped.

"Don't be ridiculous," he told her impatiently, falling silent as their barely touched salad bowls were whisked away to be replaced by steaming plates of succulent prime rib. He smoothly thanked the waiter and assured the man they needed nothing else for the time, then waited, his hazel eyes keen and penetrating, until he could speak in privacy once more. Picking up his fork and knife, he cut, chewed, and swallowed a piece of meat before continuing.

"None of this has anything to do with ego," he told her. "It all has to do with the fact we met. I want to see you again. I want to get to know you—"

76

He was interrupted by brittle laughter, and Serena realized the sound came from herself. "Oh, really, Dr. O'Neill! Don't you think the old lines are a bit silly coming now? Aren't those the usual preliminaries to 'your place or mine'? I mean, none of this is necessary—"

"Do you not listen?" Justin O'Neill broke in irritably, a man whose patience had snapped. "Or do you merely not comprehend? I said I want to get to know you. You're right," he said harshly, savaging his prime rib as he spoke. "The preliminaries were never necessary. For *either* of us. Which is rather unique, don't you think? No games, no pretenses—just something extraordinary and very beautiful. Now I think an experience like that deserves something—an admission from the man and woman involved, and mature handling."

She was trembling, Serena realized. Trembling and sawing at her meat as he did and tasting nothing when she chewed.

He is right, she thought, I keep trying to hide, to pretend that nothing had happened.

But I don't know anything about him, she thought with panic. What is he asking of me? What does he intend to give?

She forced herself to taste the prime rib. To think. To answer without anger or indignation. Still she trembled, and her words faltered.

"You're seeing me right now, Justin," she murmured. "And you're staying in my home. I—I'm not trying to lie to either of us—you're right, what happened was extraordinary, and to deny it would be to—to cheapen it. . . ." Her voice trailed away for a second. "But what happened doesn't change reality —yours or mine. No, I'm not engaged. And think what you please, my sleeping habits are my own concern. But, yes, I do have a relationship with Marc Talbot. A long relationship. I can't tell Marc to go to hell just because I met a stranger at a pond."

Serena saw his fist clench; he almost drove it against the table, then tightened his jaw, a pulse ticking, and slowly relaxed.

"Finish eating," he said curtly. "This really isn't a conversation which should take place in a public place."

Oh, God, Serena wondered, her heart pounding cruelly, where should it take place? His knees brushed against hers beneath the table, and with even that casual touch, she could remember how electrifying and powerful he could be. Heat continued to consume her, dancing along her spine, to be replaced in spurts by rampant chills. I can't be alone with him, she thought. I don't want to feel like this, like I have no control over what I really want to do.

But she was chewing as she thought. And when she set her fork down without finishing half her meal, she miserably lowered her lashes over her eyes with the admission that there was something deep within her, hiding behind a door she couldn't lock, that wanted him again, wanted just what he was asking, a chance to be known by him, to know him, to understand the keen mind within the hard-toned body.

"Finished?"

"I—" She started to speak, closed her mouth, and then nodded. He signaled for the check, left it on the table with appropriate bills, and rose before the waiter's return, reaching for her arm.

Silently she followed his escort.

He too was silent for the first few minutes he drove, and then he quietly began to speak.

"I don't believe that your relationship can be a strong one, Serena. You say you've been seeing Marc a long time. Yet you don't sleep with him, and within minutes of our meeting—"

"What makes you so damn sure about my . . . my . . ." Serena exploded her question and then stuttered in frustration.

"Your sex life?" he supplied with dry help. "You make me sure. If I hadn't been so damned stunned and jealous when I saw you last night, I would have never behaved so badly." He grimaced. "Sorry, that is one of those rather annoying male traits. Irrational jealousy, I mean. If seeing you with another man hadn't hit me like a ton of bricks, I would have never accused you of musical beds. It's obviously been a while since you've been involved with any man. You were trembling so at first, not experienced—"

"Son of a bitch!" Serena bit out furiously, pounding her palm against her forehead with a wave of humiliated rage that seemed to touch her every nerve. "First you harass me, then you change the entire thing and tell me that my performance wasn't up to your standards! Stop the car, and I damned well mean it! I can get home from here just fine on my own speed—"

"Serena, stop it!" Justin exclaimed harshly. "You're ridiculously sensitive, and perhaps I'm wording things badly—"

"I don't care!" Serena grated, gripping the seat tensely so that she didn't do something really ridiculous like attempt to smash him into the windshield. "I—don't—care! I just want to get out of this car!"

He pulled off to the shoulder of the road, but as she whirled to reach for the door handle, he swore softly and wrenched her back around to face him, holding her wrists firmly with one hand.

She sat perfectly still, staring at him with hostility seeming to come from the sky depths of her eyes.

"Let me go," she said with a deathly calm.

"I can't let you go," he said as quietly as she. "Until you listen and we reach some kind of an agreement. I want you to listen to me—"

She moaned her frustration aloud, aware that tears pricked beneath her eyelids. "Don't you understand? I don't want to listen to you; I've heard enough of what—"

"No," he persisted vehemently, leaning across the seat so that his face was within inches of hers, his heat seeming to permeate distance and touch her, magnifying the static tension. "Serena, you fool! I have never in my life known a woman like you; I have never felt that I held a creature more giving, more sensuous. There were no mechanics, Serena—no tricks of craft or trade or learning. That is all that I meant. Lord, woman, do you think I'd be sitting here like this if you didn't have me enwebbed with your unique beauty? I don't even understand this, I just know that it exists, and I won't ignore it, nor will I allow you to ignore it."

Serena stared at him, feeling her emotions pitch within her cruelly. She tried to speak and found that her lips were too dry; she tried to move her hands and realized that to ever fight him would be ludicrous—sane people didn't scuffle with weight lifters.

She had to get out. She was forced to face him. And face everything that he was saying.

Again her blood seemed to be composed of nothing but hot liquid that raced through her system, leaving her weak and shivering. She finally managed to bring words to her parched lips.

"What exactly do you want?" she demanded thickly.

"You—that's evident."

"But I . . . I can't," Serena murmured weakly. She glanced at his fingers, still wound around her wrists, and a part of her retained the amazement that he could be so massively built, yet refined in tone and delineation. "This is crazy. You're asking me for something . . . you don't believe in magic. . . . I mean . . . if there isn't magic . . . then it's simply lust, what else? And a stupid thing to throw one's life over for—"

"Listen, Serena." His impatience caused him to jerk her hands so that she refaced him with a look of shock he ignored. "How do two people ever know what they have—unless they see one another, explore feelings, learn about one another. That's all that I'm asking. I know you have a past. So do I. It would be absurd to assume either of us had been biding time in cloisters awaiting one another. But what starts any type of a relationship, Serena? Attraction—basic sexual attraction."

"No," Serena protested. "Friendship can lead to attraction—"

His laughter, as tense as his hold and his eyes, cut her off. "If you believe that you're going to find this wonderful attraction for your friend when it's been missing all along, I'm afraid you're mistaken."

He was right, her mind screamed. She had hidden behind her

80

widowhood with Marc as nothing more than an excuse. She had enjoyed Marc's companionship; she had enjoyed the warmth he offered; she had even enjoyed his kisses. She was human and she needed that warmth.

No, what am I thinking? Marc cares for me; he is there and he will always be there. And this ridiculously overwhelming sexual thing cannot last. If it wasn't magic, it was the trees, the pond, the earth. It will end, and I would have thrown away something so good.

He released her hands suddenly. "You're a coward, Serena," he said, his tone venting his disappointment.

She automatically rubbed her wrists. "I'm a coward because I should drop everything—and run off with you tonight? We could just elope, right? I mean we're both so sure of this thing—"

Something, a chilling shield, blanked the emotion from his eyes as he stared straight into the darkness. "I'm not a big believer in marriage, Serena. I—"

"Oh, great!" she spat out incredulously, "Now I do have it! Turn my life around so that I can be your summer mistress! What a deal, Dr. O'Neill. Wonderful!"

He turned on her again, and this time his fingers threaded her hair, their touch so pleasing it was painful. "I'm asking you to take a chance, Serena. The same chance I'm taking. I can't give you guarantees—anymore than you can give them to me! At least act honestly. I went into Boston that night to end things, Serena. I didn't know if I would ever see you again, but being with you was enough for me to know that I couldn't continue with a relationship that offered less than what we had—as strangers!" His grip on her hair tensed, then relaxed slightly as he groaned. One hand remained tangled in her hair, the other slid down her back, pressing her to him. His face burrowed against her neck, and she almost cried out with the fire that swept her flesh just with the touch of his breath. Then his lips caressed the bare skin, a brand that seared all memory, all argument from her mind. A soft moan escaped her, and she brought her arms around him, feeling the clean cut of the soft hair at the nape of his neck. Dizziness eclipsed everything as she clung to him. Fever and weakness overcame her as his teeth grazed her throat and the lobe of her ear, sending wave after wave of jolting fire down her spine. She loved the play of her fingers over his shoulders, his back. He was so rigid, so tense, yet so hot and alive beneath the touch of her fingertips.

"Justin," she breathed, and it was a lost cry; she was aware only that it felt wonderful and right to say his name.

It was incredible that he could hold her completely in the confines of the sports car, but she felt melded to him.

I will promise anything, she thought deliriously.

His mouth found hers, softly. He drew a moist whisper of a pattern with the tip of his tongue about her lips. He kissed her eyelids, and then his lips returned to hers hungrily, parting them, devouring them, only to draw away again to taste the flesh near them, making her reach in return to seek his mouth with the tip of her tongue . . . and again be consumed.

"I need you," he murmured, his mouth still against hers, and it was as if the world itself had been obscured. At that moment she had no idea of where she was, nor did she care. With him it didn't matter. There was a plane above all else. It burned like a raging fire, but it was a place of clouds, where all was filled with blazing light, where tempest still meant security. It was where she had always been meant to be; almost as if she had been there before . . . as if she knew . . .

It was all in his arms, and she held to him in that plane, arching as he touched her, loving his demanding hands upon her back, massaging her breast, cradling her throat with tenderness so his lips could more fully find her. And as she drifted in that plane, she thought vaguely that no matter how absurd a thought it might be, she loved him.

In one aspect he had been wrong. All her life she had been waiting for him. Even the gentle love she had shared in marriage had been but a step to this point. She loved him. . . . It was instant recognition.

A soft whimpered sigh escaped her as his fingers ran down her spine. And then she suddenly found herself untouched; he released her and shifted his body fully back into the driver's seat.

For seconds she felt bewildered—totally bereft and confused. She stared at him blankly in the darkness, stunned by the burning anger in his hazel scrutiny.

"I'll give you a week," he said curtly.

Serena felt the delicious heat drain from her instantly to be replaced by a cold fury. His every action had been calculated; the psychologist had played upon her body and mind as a parent might manipulate a child. She realized that she was sitting in the bucket seat of a sports car and that her clothing was a ruffled disaster. Her hair was the wild evidence that she had been doing exactly what she had been doing. Petting like a high school senior in a car. And if he had continued with his expert administrations, she wouldn't have even thought of where she was. She would have given in to any demand.

She trembled with a furious rage as she adjusted her clothing, forgetting in her anger that she had admitted the raw emotion that dug like a claw within her. "Take me back to my car," she demanded with a vehement quiet. "Now, please!"

Justin obligingly started the car. He drove in silence for a moment and then said just as quietly, "Did you hear me, Serena? I said I'd give you one week."

"I heard you," she said grimly, and stared stonily out the windshield. With great effort she controlled the screaming turmoil of her mind and half turned to him coolly. "You'll give me a week. So just what happens at the end of that week?"

He glanced at her, that challenging half smile on his lips, and that blazing and deadly serious intensity in his eyes.

"I come for you," he said simply.

What does that mean? she shrieked silently to herself. But the words wouldn't form on her lips. She just sat as they drove, eyes ahead, hands clenched tightly in her lap. The crescents of her nails dug little half-moons into her palms, but she didn't feel them.

Her own car sat before the darkened museum in the silent street. As Justin parked beside it, she instantly jerked the door handle and bolted. "I'll follow you to the inn," he called, making no attempt to stop her.

"There's no need," she called back.

Her tires screeched, her car jerked insanely. She wanted to leave him behind in the dust.

But she realized she was behaving absurdly like an adolescent, and she forced herself to slow down and drive responsibly. When she reached the inn, she exited her car and ran for the doorway without bothering to lock it, praying that the entryway would be empty and that she wouldn't be compelled to chatter politely with her guests or Martha.

The old inn was silent. Serena stepped down the hall to the main stairway, then felt a prickling at the nape of her neck.

With her hand on the bannister, she turned, seeing the rear wall of the parlor from her vantage point of height.

The portrait, Marc's painting of Eleanora, had been hung above the fireplace.

Beautiful blue eyes seemed to stare back at her sadly.

"Oh, hell!" Serena muttered aloud. She heard Justin reaching the door and twisting the knob as she spun from the too familiar eyes of Eleanora to race the rest of the way up the stairs.

In her room she closed the door behind her and leaned against it as if she had been pursued. "What the hell is happening?" she whispered aloud.

With trembling fingers she stripped off her clothing, allowing it to fall unheeded to the floor, and walked into the bathroom, sitting in the tub as the water filled it. She liberally laced the water with the rose softening beads she loved, thinking stupidly that she could once more erase the scent of him from her body.

But her efforts were useless. Dressed in a gown and curled into her bed with the covers clutched to her chest, she found herself staring at the back wall, and at the panel that hid the rear stairwell.

Eleanora's stairwell.

She didn't want to think about the tragedy of a long dead ancestor that night, but it would be preferable to fill her mind with thoughts of the lady than of Justin O'Neill.

But even staring at the panel, absurdly, made her think of Justin. "I hate him," she moaned aloud with soft vehemence. "He has made a mess of my life; he has made a mess of *me!*"

But when she finally slept, a smile curved her lips. Her dreams were of Justin, and in her dreams they met by the pond.

And the air was cool and fresh and fragrant and the benign branches of the sheltering trees were their harbor as they lay naked together . . . laughing and loving.

Because she did love him. She had loved him forever and forever.

CHAPTER FIVE

"Serena. Serena. *Serena!*"

The calling of her name finally penetrated her mind so thoroughly that she jumped and sent a dozen invoices flying and floating to the floor around her.

Susan sighed with exasperation and bent to retrieve the papers.

"Do you know, Serena, if you're not interested in becoming a witch and joining a coven, you should take up yoga. Or something. Anything! Your nerves are strung like a kite!"

"I'm not really nervous," Serena protested, bending to retrieve the papers with Susan. She met Susan's skeptical eyes as they both crawled about on the floor. "All right, I am nervous. But I'm always nervous. Some people are just nervous people!"

Susan laughed. "Want to tell me the problem? Maybe I could mix up a potion that *would* help!"

With the last of the papers retrieved, Serena sat back down behind the desk with a sigh. "I don't think so, Susan. I wouldn't want to ruin your standing as a *good* witch!"

"It's that hulk of a psychologist, isn't it?"

Serena glanced at Susan sharply. It had been five days since Justin had appeared at the museum—and neither she nor Susan had mentioned him since.

"Why do you say that?" Serena queried her friend warily.

Susan chuckled wickedly. "Because there are vibes about that man, honey. It doesn't take a witch to tune in on him! What I can't figure out is how you're having a problem! If he winked at me—"

"Susan," Serena murmured, "you're forgetting about Marc."

"Ah—hah!" Susan pounced. "So then you admit that the doctor has made advances!"

Serena blushed and tapped her pencil against the desk. Advances! If Susan only knew. . . .

If Susan knew, she would drive her crazy. She would see all kinds of things in the situation. She would chatter all day about the beauty of destiny and the wonders of the magic of the earth.

"Yes," Serena muttered dryly, "I guess you could say he's made a few advances."

"Then, sweetie," Susan murmured, her lovely brown eyes huge and wide, "why are you a wreck? The man is . . . one of a kind! Polite and cordial and civil and suave, and yet a walking mass of sexuality! You don't get to see bodies like that in the magazines most of the time!"

"Susan," Serena said primly, "what about Marc? He may not be Hercules, but he's a hell of a nice guy, and we've been together for a year now. He wants marriage and children and the lot, and we both love Salem, and we respect one another! We almost never argue—"

"Sounds like you're trying to write him a résumé for a good job," Susan observed.

"Oh, Susan, I don't know!" Serena laughed. "Marc's driving me just as nuts as our illustrious Dr. O'Neill. They're both driving me nuts! Marc is running around the house with tape recorders tapping the walls and trying to convince me my house is haunted! On Monday he came in with that old painting of Eleanora, and I think he's trying to convince me I'm some kind of a reincarnation of her! This morning he arrived before I was awake and started prowling around the attic—tapping walls again. Then he goes tearing out of the house screaming something about his 'proof.' "

Susan laughed so hard she clutched her middle. "Well, Serena, maybe the old inn is haunted! If spirits do come back, that would be the place!"

"Susan! I've lived in the Golden Hawk all my life! I never even heard the boards creak."

Susan shrugged. "You're funny, Serena. You're all logic, but you don't mind having a witch for a best friend!"

Serena shrugged in return. "To me, Sue, your witchcraft is like a religion. You're a sweet lady trying to do nice things, and although I'm not a 'witch,' you have to admit I know more about the practices through the ages than most of your coven!"

Susan was staring at her. "You want to know something funny, Serena? That's what your Dr. O'Neill said to me—almost word for word."

Serena stiffened. In the past days she had avoided Justin like the plague, and she had done a fair job of staying out of his way. Only now and then had they run into one another, and she had immediately torn her eyes from his each time, trying to still the violent trembling that assailed her with his piercing, knowledgeable stare. He hadn't come near the museum; when had he spoken to Susan?

"He showed up right after you left last night," Susan said, answering the unspoken question. "He knew last night was one of our high holidays, and he asked if he might come and quietly observe the ritual."

"Oh," Serena murmured, biting her lip at the stab of jealousy that seemed to dig at her like a knife.

"Don't 'oh' me, Serena!" Susan laughed. "You may be claiming loyalty to Marc, but I can read between the lines. And nothing happened. The man has no interest in me except a friendly one! And what a pity that is! I wouldn't be wishy-washy in return, and that's a fact!"

"Susan," Serena protested, "that's part of my point. I don't trust a man like Justin O'Neill. He's . . . he's too physical. Part of his interest could just be . . . well, the challenge of the thing. I mean, he has to know his build is . . . dynamite, I guess. And you don't get a build like that without working at it, and to work at it that strenuously, it must have a lot to do with a monumental ego—"

"Un-unh," Susan corrected, perching on the side of the desk. "I can tell you exactly why he looks like Schwartzenegger from the neck down."

"Oh?"

"There goes that 'oh' again!" Susan chuckled cheerfully. "See, if you took the time to get to know the man, you might take that snooty little nose out of the air."

"Oh, really?"

"Really!"

Serena waited for Susan to go on, then realized her friend was purposely baiting her. She laughed. "Okay, Susan, why the body-build?"

"Polio."

"Polio?" Serena repeated with an incredulous frown.

"Yep, he was half-crippled as a child, and the doctors told his parents that the future was up to him. He had to learn to work on his muscles—and he's grateful now for his health. Says he never takes health or the body for granted." Susan paused for a minute. "He is one great person, Serena. They don't come in that mold often. A sharp-as-a-whip Goliath."

Serena reflected silently for a second, chewing the stub of her pen. Sue was right; they didn't come in that mold often.

So if they came and left, they left devastation. It had taken her what seemed like forever to mourn her husband; she had slowly and solidly built the respect that she and Marc shared.

Did she dare take a chance?

She rubbed her temple with her fingers. "We're back to the same issue, Susan. What about Marc? What do I say? 'Gee, Marc, would you mind waiting around for a while so I can see if I can make it with Dr. O'Neill, the brilliant jock who just kind of swept in?' "

"Serena! I'm surprised at you!" Susan chastised. "You have to make up your mind about Marc for what the two of you have —not for what you might or might not be able to exchange it for!"

89

Serena sighed. "You're right, Sue. I . . . I just don't know. I feel so terrible."

"That's not the way to look at it either!" Susan warned. "You can't keep dating Marc and leading him on to believe you might love him one day just so that you don't hurt him! The deceit would be far worse in the end, especially since it's obvious you're as drawn to O'Neill as he is to you."

Serena sniffed a little bitterly. "You make it sound so logical and easy."

"That's because I'm giving the advice. Now if it were for myself, I'd just cook up a few good potions for both of them! And a few appropriate spells could be chanted. One to get rid of a man, and one to hook a husband."

Serena decided to forget her bookkeeping for the day. She shuffled her papers together and stood with a wan smile for Susan. "Thanks, kid, but that's another thing that makes me a bit nervous. Doctor Hulk doesn't believe in marriage."

"Ahh . . . but, we'll hit him with magic!"

"He doesn't believe in magic, either!" Serena laughed dryly. "Oh, I don't know, Susan! I just don't know."

But I guess I have to figure something out soon, she added silently to herself. Her week was almost up.

Maybe I should take up yoga or meditation, she thought as she unsuccessfully attempted to fit her house key into the lock. She dropped the key and bent to retrieve it, then smiled awkwardly as Mr. Donnesy, sprightly and charming as his wife, opened the door for her.

"Thought it would be you at this time, Serena." He smiled, his gray eyes bright behind his wire-rimmed glasses. "You certainly have been all thumbs lately, missy."

Serena smiled weakly. "Thanks, Mr. Donnesy. I'm sorry if I disturbed you."

"Not at all," he said, chuckling, "and I'll show you why!"

He slipped an arm through hers and led her into the parlor, where his wife and the Bakers were deeply involved in the board game Risk. Mr. Donnesy patted his wife's shoulder affectionately, and she absently clutched his hand.

"I don't know about Mildred," Mr. Donnesy said with a sigh and a shake of his head. "Sweet woman till you hand her a pair of dice. It's like opening Pandora's box." His voice lowered in disbelieving complaint. "I had all of North America. My armies were in Australia, and it almost looked as if I had Europe in the bag. Then *she* comes along like the wrath of God!"

"There, there, dear," Mildred Donnesy soothed, glancing up from the board to give Serena a radiant smile. "Poor man was suffering from delusions of grandeur. I had to take him down a peg."

"Ouch!" Pierce Baker suddenly murmured. "You think you're having problems! Mildred just snuffed me out of Asia!"

Serena laughed and started to excuse herself, then decided she might as well prepare herself for the evening. "Who's here tonight, Mr. Donnesy? Did Marc ever come back after he left this morning?" Unintentionally she lowered her eyes. "And what about Dr. O'Neill?"

"The gang's all here," Mildred Donnesy said, shaking the dice within their little container. "Ahhhh-ha! Double sixes! That wipes you out, Pierce."

"Heaven forbid!" Pierce groaned. "The world is in the hands of two fanatical females!"

Pierce Baker was as plump as a Santa Claus, while Giles Donnesy was slender as a string bean. The two men together were an absurdly distinguished Laurel and Hardy. Shaking his head in the bewilderment that only recently plagued Giles, Pierce left the table.

"A delightful man, that New York professor!" he told Serena with a wink. "Giles and I spent the afternoon with him, studying transcripts of the witchcraft trials. The things he pointed out I've never even thought of before! Brilliant, really brilliant."

Brilliant, Serena thought with dry bitterness. Brilliant, just brilliant. It would be so nice if someone, just one person, would decide that Justin O'Neill was an obnoxious bore.

Serena smiled. "Where is everyone else now?"

Pierce shrugged. "That young man of yours has been prowling around the hidden staircase all day. Justin is probably still swimming."

"Down at the pond," Giles supplied.

Damn him! Serena thought. Not only had he been making her a wreck all week, he was destroying her greatest pleasure of the summer. Instinct had warned her to stay away from the pond, and instinct had been proven right. She had learned from Martha that O'Neill swam daily.

Was he waiting for her to reappear? she wondered with a shiver suddenly raking down her spine. If he were, he had a long wait.

"Good luck ruling the world, ladies!" she said to Mildred and Gayle, adding to their husbands, "Thanks, guys," before leaving them to their pursuits.

The men gave her cheerful waves and moved back to the table to cheer on their wives. As she had so often done in the days since its arrival, Serena paused in the hallway to stare at the picture above the mantel. Eleanora Hawk stared back with her same sad smile.

Serena hurried into the kitchen, frowning as she saw that Martha was not busy preparing dinner. "Martha?"

The screen door to the yard suddenly breezed open as Martha bustled in, smiling as she saw Serena. "Hello, dear, nice day?"

Serena shrugged, "The usual, Martha." She hesitated for a second. "Are we eating late tonight? What would you like me to do?"

"Not a thing, dear. We're all set. We'll be eating shortly, just as soon as Justin gets back from his swim."

"Oh." The tone of Serena's voice sounded her confusion.

"A barbecue, dear!" Martha laughed. "Salad's in the fridge, and the corn has been grilling a half hour. I mentioned this morning what a lovely idea it would be, and of course the Donnesys and Bakers were all for it. Justin offered to act as chef, and," she added a bit acidly, "Marc offered to help. Since he's been consuming Golden Hawk food all week, I certainly thought it fitting for him to cook!"

"I think I'll have a cold beer," Serena murmured.

Oh, boy, a barbecue, she thought, feeling a headache coming on. She kept her smile up as she sailed across the room to duck into the refrigerator and rummage through its varied contents. The screen door opened again as she balanced on the balls of her feet. Grabbing a lite, she glanced up.

It was Justin, clad in cutoffs and sandals only, his hair wet and slicked back from his forehead, a towel slung around his neck.

He glanced down just as she glanced up.

Serena stared at him blankly for a second, her mind and heart racing. He looked much as he had that first day at the pond—broad, tanned chest sleek with moisture, suddenly towering over her from out of nowhere.

She stood quickly, disliking the disadvantage of her position. "Good evening, Dr. O'Neill," she murmured coolly.

He inclined his head with a lifted brow. "Good evening, Mrs. Loren." He glanced from her to Martha. "I'll start the steaks now, if you wish, Martha."

"Wonderful," Martha replied. "Serena, the meat is there, under the wax paper. Bring it outside for Justin, will you please? I'll go see how the fate of the world is going and let them all know dinner is about ready."

Justin disappeared out the screen door and Martha swung her way out to the main part of the house. Gritting her teeth, Serena followed Justin with the meat.

She dropped the steaks on the portable wrought iron counter by the grill. "Can I get you anything else, Dr. O'Neill?"

"No," he replied, his gaze long and assessing. "But you can keep me company."

"I . . . uh . . ."

"Yes?"

Serena shrugged and stood silently near him.

The steaks sizzled as they hit the grill. "I've missed you at the pond," Justin said casually.

"I've missed the pond," she replied, her reproach for his intrusion of her privacy evident. "I thought you jogged," she added ungraciously. "Isn't that sufficient for your daily exercise?"

He glanced at her with narrowed eyes. "Is it just me, Serena, or do you hold all runners with equal contempt."

She hesitated a second, lowering her eyes. Then she raised them again. "Nothing personal, Dr. O'Neill. I'm not crazy about jogging. My husband had a heart attack and dropped dead while jogging."

His eyes didn't lower from hers. "I'm sorry, Serena," he said quietly.

She blinked and her eyes slipped past him to stare unseeingly at the forest which surrounded the inn. For a moment she had felt a strange catch in her heart, not for the husband she had lost, but for the man who had been costing her sleep by his very existence.

When he had spoken to her, she had felt that tug of familiarity, that rightness, about being near him.

I do love him, she thought. I love the way he moves. I love his mind. I love the quirk in his brows, that fathomless storm that can darken his eyes. I don't know him, but I do know him. I know his moods, I know his needs, I know his love. . . .

"Serena! There you are!"

Marc bounded from the house, notepad and pen in hand. He rushed to Serena, gripped her shoulders, and brushed her lips with a hasty kiss. "Darling, just wait till I spring today's surprise on you!"

"I can hardly," Serena murmured, uncomfortable with the awareness that Justin was watching her. She pulled from Marc's hold subtly and smiled so there would be no repulse to her action. "What is it?"

"Oh, I can't show you now! But I will in just a few days." He fell silent as if he realized suddenly that they weren't alone. "You'll enjoy my discovery, too, O'Neill. It was a real find."

"I'll be waiting," Justin said politely, and Serena noticed that he watched Marc not with jealousy, but with a patient tolerance.

"Listen," Marc continued apologetically, "I know I offered

to help with the barbecue, but I really need to get into Boston. Would you mind if I copped out, Justin?"

"No problem," Justin replied evenly.

Marc rubbed his chin with a grimace and turned his attention back to Serena. "God, honey, I'm sorry, I just realized this is Friday night. I should be taking you someplace."

Serena felt her breath coming short. The pain of her deception and hypocrisy was suddenly staggering. "It's all right, Marc," she said, her voice just above a whisper. He had been in such a whirl all week he had never noticed she had been avoiding him too. "I have to open the museum tomorrow anyway. You know how I need my sleep."

"Serena, you're a gem," Marc said, stepping forward to quickly kiss her brow. He started to walk across the lawn, then suddenly turned back. "Hey, Justin! Thanks again for all the copies of the trial transcripts! I never knew they had so much on the Hawks in them!"

Justin didn't reply; he waved his answer. Serena waited until Marc rounded the whitewashed corner of the house to speak. "You've helped Marc with research?" she asked.

He shrugged. "I had to have it all myself, so I just made two copies of everything I had duplicated. Get the plates, will you? Everyone ordered rare."

Serena turned and headed for the kitchen. She ducked inside and found Martha had left a large serving platter on the counter. Clutching it, she walked back out to the barbecue.

Justin glanced at her for a second, then began stabbing the meat to transfer it from flame to stoneware. "Well, 'gem,' " he murmured, "I see you haven't sat down with Marc for an honest conversation yet."

Serena drew in a breath. His eyes found hers again. "You can't run forever, you know."

She clasped her hands to still her trembling fingers. "You know," she repeated in the same blasé tone, "if it weren't for Tom, Dr. O'Neill, I wouldn't even need to talk. I would ask you to take your patronage elsewhere."

"Tom?" his brows lifted high. "Another poor dangling sap, Mrs. Loren?"

She smiled vaguely, remembering that he had no idea of who Tom might be. His voice had sounded gruff, which gave her a little thrill of pleasure. Inexperienced, was she? she thought with a laugh. He had been so damned certain of her—it was fun for a moment to allow him to think he just might have been wrong. . . .

His fingers suddenly clutched her upper arm, and in that simple gesture she saw the pulse and bulge of a dozen tight muscles across his chest.

Then she saw the piercing demand in his eyes, and triumph fled away as she heard herself explaining. "My brother, Justin. Tom Hawk. He owns half of the inn. And," she added bitterly, "although he leaves the management to me, he loves it dearly. And I doubt that he'd appreciate me kicking you out. Therefore I have tolerated your presence."

She panicked for a brief moment, holding her breath, her eyes widening. She felt a bit like a canary in a gilded cage, chirping away in a cat's claw. She had seen him angry, but never furious, and it occurred to her belatedly that in a full-fledged temper he would be terrible to see.

But she began inhaling air again as she saw that her remark hadn't made him angry. To the contrary, he laughed and his whisper brushed her ear. "Mrs. Loren, when are you going to stop lying to yourself?"

She didn't reply. She heard the chattering of Martha and the inn's other guests as the screen door slammed behind them and they all moved out to the lawn. Justin's eyes rose from hers and focused on the group coming up from behind her. "Rare as ordered," he called cheerfully.

Serena ran back into the kitchen for the beer she had never had a chance to drink.

To her surprise she enjoyed the evening. The seven of them sat about the wooden picnic table, and conversation never flagged. Serena learned that Justin O'Neill was a man with

96

widespread and diverse interests. He listened to the Donnesys' and Bakers' tales of travel and laughingly contributed a few of his own. He loved museums of any kind, she discovered, just as he loved activity, and if something were brought up about which he knew little, he readily admitted it and listened.

It was a long and leisurely dinner, with Serena the only silent one at the table.

When at long last the coals were quenched and the plates collected, the older couples yawned and said their good nights. But as Giles Donnesy reached the screen door, he paused to turn back to Justin. "I'll work up those notes for you tomorrow morning, young man! Don't you worry!"

"Thanks, Mr. Donnesy!" Justin replied smoothly. "I appreciate it."

Serena glared at Justin but said nothing until Martha had followed the Donnesys inside.

"What do you think you're doing?" she demanded. "Making that nice old man spend his summer vacation reading books for you! You have no right to expect that of anyone, Doctor, especially since you are supposed to be so damned brilliant in your field!"

She should have instantly realized the answer when it came to her with his contemptuous stare.

Oh, Lord, she thought, he didn't need help from anyone. He probably had a mind like a damned computer. All he had done was made her older guests feel wonderful. He had made them feel respected and needed, and he had given them the glory of knowing that their own minds were as bright and beautiful as when their bodies were young.

Serena clutched the garbage she had been collecting tightly in her hands. "I'm sorry," she said quickly, and then, before she could burst into tears of misery and confusion, she fled into the house.

In her room she took two aspirin, and then took two more. She drew a very hot bath and plunged into it, praying that the mist above the water could make the rough edges of her whirling mind begin to blur.

Justin bathed quickly in cold water and then poured a generous portion of whiskey into a cup of the coffee Martha provided him nightly in a thermos so that he could work at night undisturbed.

But he had no interest in working tonight. He stared at his meticulous notes on the trials and the Mathers in particular with absent distaste. His concentration was simply shot. He slipped the cover over his typewriter and prowled his room in his robe, raking his fingers repeatedly through his hair.

It had been his torture knowing that she was just a few doors away. And now he had to wonder what the hell had been the matter with him to threaten her or offer ultimatums.

Although he had spent his life studying human behavior, he had no explanation for his own.

She was simply a fever in his blood. When he closed his eyes at night he saw her, the sparkling violet eyes, the waving mass of chestnut hair, the simple beauty of her curving smile.

And, he thought wryly, the simple beauty of her other curves, too.

But though he longed to hold those curves, there was more to his obsession. He had never been so affected by a woman, and he was still a little stunned. He loved to merely watch her walk across a room. The soft sound of her voice seemed to permeate his soul. He loved the keen glitter of interest which would so often sharpen her eyes.

He stopped his pacing and drained his spiked coffee, then lay upon his bed, staring up at the ceiling.

I love her mind, he thought.

Sure, man, you love her mind. That's why you're lying here wondering if you ought to try sleeping in the bathtub with the water high on cold.

But I do, he thought wryly. I love her mind. I want her so badly that I can't function, but part of that wanting is because I love all that is mirrored in those beautiful eyes.

He had spent his days subtly querying anyone he could about her. And as he had expected, he had only learned nice things.

She had adored her husband; they had been a marvelous couple, always doing things together. She had never even noticed the glances of other men.

And when the Donnesys had been injured in a car accident together, Serena had flown to be with them so that they could come home rather than be confined in the hospital, old and alone.

So many things he had learned about her. Beautiful things.

Too bad, he thought dryly, that someone hadn't mentioned her brother. He had almost blown the whole thing tonight when she mentioned "Tom."

Oh, God, he thought, I am obsessed. I'm in love, and I didn't think I really believed in love.

I even want children with her.

Jenny, he thought then, I wonder what she'll think of Jenny. She doesn't even know I have a daughter.

Justin stood up and glanced at the paneling to the right of his bed. He turned away from it.

He had been exploring since he arrived—and discovered the catch to the hidden door. It led to the hidden stairway.

And the stairway veered down, and then back up.

To Serena's room.

Get away from there, he grumbled silently to himself.

He started pacing again. Damn, but she was different. He winced with the memory of his last encounter with Denise at the restaurant. She had flown into a rage first, then into a fit of very dramatic tears when he had said it was over between them. She had assumed it was another woman—and at that time, she had only been partly right. He had realized that he couldn't continue the empty, shallow relationship any longer. But even as she had cried, he had wondered how many tears had actually been shed for him. The tears had faded too quickly and become another rage in which she had informed him that his career would falter without her. She had spurred him on; she had made him what he was.

He suddenly discovered that he was not only staring at the

paneling again, but that he had stopped his pacing directly in front of the catch.

I can't, he thought. I gave her a week.

Yeah, and what happens when she ignores me, which it appears she has every intention of doing?

She wants me. I know it! I know it when I touch her, when I see her eyes.

I need her.

I can't go sneaking into her room.

Well, I sure as hell can't knock. She won't let me in.

If I don't touch her, feel her next to me, I'll go crazy. I can't sleep because she's in my dreams and I wake up aching.

I cannot go through that panel.

It wouldn't be right; it wouldn't be fair.

He stared at the paneling as seconds ticked by. Then his fingers reached out and ran slowly down the board.

The hell with fair.

His fingers found the hollow section, and he pressed. A section of the wall revolved neatly to reveal the old wooden spiral stairs.

He paused only long enough to fetch his flashlight from the nightstand drawer, then he moved into the staircase. He cursed as he smashed his head against the sloping ceiling. "Damned thing was built for midgets," he muttered beneath his breath.

He had to follow the spiral down to the first floor, then find the spring in the dead-end panel. The well was two-sided—two avenues of escape, he assumed. If one was discovered, the other might still go unnoticed.

He found the second spring and entered the tiny enclosure which led both outside and up—to Serena's room. "You've come this far, O'Neill," he told himself silently. "No chickening out now."

He trained his light on the second spiral of steps and hunched his back over to prevent another clunk on the head. When he reached the top, he allowed his fingers to grope a third time.

And just as surely they found the third spring. A panel quietly slid—and gave him entrance.

She wasn't in the bedroom, but he saw the light in the bathroom and heard the splash and ripple of water.

He closed the panel behind him and leaned against it, absently crossing his arms over his chest as his eyes scanned her room.

Woven blue throw rugs adorned the highly polished floor, and the walls were papered in a lattice pattern of a complementing shade. The drapes were white and elegantly sheer, as was the spread on the queen-size bed. Her toiletries were neatly displayed on an antique dresser. Her penchant for her town was clearly in evidence; little "kitchen" witches dangled from the ceiling along with a huge potted fern. A TV/stereo cabinet sat across from the bed, filled with a variety of albums and tapes. He wanted to study every album, to know her taste in music. He was so hungry for any little scrap of knowledge about her.

She's going to freak out when she sees you, O'Neill. Scream her head off and order you out of her house, brother or no.

I have to be here. I can't stay away anymore.

I have to have her.

A slight sound drew his wandering gaze sharply back to the bathroom door.

She stood before him, a huge white towel wrapped around her torso.

Her eyes were huge in her face, shimmering their unique blue-violet. Her hair cascaded in heavy waves about her ivory shoulders, and her lips were parted in incredulous surprise.

He had never seen her more beautiful, nor more vulnerable.

Nor had he ever felt such a pounding in his own system; a drumbeat that had to be obeyed. The fire for her that raged through him was everything; it was his pulse, his very existence at that moment.

"You don't need any more time," he heard himself drawl harshly. "We both know you're mine. And I've come for you."

Their eyes were locked across the room in a staggering tension that surpassed that of the heavens with the coming of a storm.

Fool, he hissed to himself, idiot.

"Serena!" he demanded aloud.

And for a second—or was it an eternity—time stood still.

CHAPTER SIX

At first sight of the man in her bedroom, Serena almost screamed. But she choked back the sound.

It didn't seem so terribly strange that he was there. And it didn't take an Einstein to realize he had aptly discovered the passageways and staircases that wound within the house.

A thousand things raced through her mind as she stared at him. Thoughts of how he looked, leaning against the paneling, arms across his chest . . . casual, yet challenging, demanding, seeking. For all the world as if he belonged.

My week isn't up, she thought in panic. But did it matter? Did anything matter?

She wanted and needed him as she had never wanted or needed anyone in her life. Her eyes were held by his; there was that goading, self-assured challenge in his intense gaze.

But there was more. That look that merged with hers, as if all were undeniable, as if theirs had been a rendezvous appointed by destiny. He knew no more than she why the obsession was so blinding, but just as she, he accepted the tempestuous storm of passionate desire that brought them here, face-to-face, against anything and everything.

And then greater than wonder came the knowledge that she

had been a fool. So seldom in a lifetime was it possible to find love, to give love, and she had tried to deny it.

And he was there, standing before her. Like he belonged, because he did belong.

Serena barely heard his words. The tone didn't matter; the words didn't matter. There was naked need in his eyes beneath the veneer of demand. She echoed a tiny cry, and forgetting all else, she raced across the room to hurtle herself into his arms, burying her face against his neck and shoulder, clinging to him as the hammer of his heart became a drumbeat within her system.

He held her a moment, pressing her close. He ran his fingers slowly and soothingly through her hair.

"Serena . . ." he whispered, and the sound was rich with longing. She tilted her head back and met his eyes, and saw both the fires and the anguish. She lowered her lashes and burrowed against him again, rubbing her cheek against the crisp hairs that grew high on his broad chest beneath the collarbones. His hands spanned the small of her back and rose to her shoulders to draw her back an inch. He met her eyes again, and his were soft now with unspoken understanding. He reached for the folded knot that held the towel to her and released it; the towel fell to the floor at her feet. Serena hesitantly touched upon the belt of his robe, her fingers becoming surer. But as the belt gave and the robe slipped open, he groaned and crushed her against him once more, and the fires mounted as the softness of her flesh was kissed by the rougher quality of his. She could feel the pillar of his thigh hard against her, the hair of his calves teasing hers, the magnificent chest warming her breasts until her nipples felt ignited by blue flame.

His fingers raked her silken hair, and her face was raised to his. He kissed the snow-white arch of her throat first, groans of need escaping him in whispers that were incoherent words. Then his lips rained about her face, avoiding her mouth until a last sweet moment, then devouring it hungrily. His passion was a wind that knew no course; it swept with driven abandon.

104

Serena was at first weak against it, accepting, seeking just to be swept up with the storm.

But the fire became a flame that soared high, a guide to her quivering needs and senses. She played her nails over his chest, savoring the sensations she received by sensitized fingertips. She pressed herself against him and lowered her body against his, raking lips and teeth and darting tongue over his male nipples, over his hard trembling musculature, down to his lean trim belly. She cradled his hips with her hands, finding enticement in the sleekness of the man, in the mere feel of his skin, in the intricacies of vital heated flesh.

"Serena . . ." He groaned her name, and his hands wound into her hair. He lowered himself in front of her and swept her into his arms, massaging her shoulders with lips of liquid fire as his hands moved along her back to lift her buttocks. Her back arched to his touch as his mouth traced downward to caress her breasts, his teeth and tongue playing upon the nipples with a suctioning demand that brought a fervent moan to her lips and a shooting weakness through her body. She collapsed against him, and he tucked one arm beneath her knees and one about her shoulders to lift her high against him and carry her to the bed, his whispered caresses filling her all the while. He laid her down and shook his robe from his shoulders to join her, but as her long slender arms reached for him, he ignored them, bending over her to reverently consume her length with his eyes, then touch her gently with roughened fingertips that added kindling to the fire already ignited within her. He drew a circle upon the smooth flesh of her abdomen and then bent to kiss it, repeating the design with his tongue. She was tense beneath him, writhing at his touch, catching her breath in tiny gasps. He drew his patterns low over her hips, teasing the heart of her need in a skim, and brushing the tender flesh on her inner thighs. She tensed anew with a moan, and her nails dug into his shoulders. He probed firmly then between her thighs, and for a second she stiffened with trembling tension. And then she opened to him sweetly, flesh quivering, whispering his name with a sob that was choked from her lips. He laid himself between her legs, his hand sliding down the length of one as he loved her and teased her before bringing his weight carefully above her and staring down into her face.

Her eyes were closed, but now they too opened to him. He was met by a dazzling sapphire so stunning he caught his belabored breath. Her hands laced around his neck. "I love you," she murmured with a quiver.

He closed his own eyes for a second, as if to retain the vision forever. He opened them and whispered in return, "Precious beauty, precious witch, I love you too. . . ."

He felt the silk of her legs as they wound around him. And he entered her slowly despite the raging tide of consuming need within. He savored every second moving within her until he was fully embraced, and she was filled, gasping his name with the sensation.

Only then did the passion break, the storm surge. A glorious rhythm that knew no bounds, a fusion of heat and undulating need that soared like the wind. Wave after wave of increasing tension hit, only to ride and crest again, higher, stronger. Through it all he held her to him, pulling her tight, releasing her slightly to seek a breast and devour it with passion. But when the urgency of the highest crest was reached, he crushed her against him, face burrowed to neck, lips pressed to her ear as his cry of coming ecstasy shuddered out in a breeze that spurred her own. They held together tightly, until her strangled gasp of trembling rapture released him.

And then there was that moment of wondrous awe, of spellbinding beauty as their bodies radiated in the fulfillment.

He shifted his weight from her but held her still, supporting her against himself, his chin resting upon the top of her head as he soothed her spine with his fingers.

I cannot live without him, Serena thought simply, watching her fingers where they lay resting over his damp chest. She closed her eyes, not wanting to think, but merely luxuriating in the feel of being beside him, still so much a part of him.

They lay silent for a time, then he shifted to touch her chin

106

and arch her face upward. His eyes were gentle, yet dark and brooding.

"I do love you, Serena," he said softly.

She smiled, then a darkness came to her own eyes. "I love you," she replied. "I . . . I love you so much that it scares me silly."

He didn't dispute her; he stroked her hair.

"Any emotion this strong and overwhelming is scary, Serena. I'm scared myself. I never knew that love could be so consuming. I've wanted you and needed you so badly, I was about to take desperate measures."

Serena lifted a brow and inclined her head toward the paneling.

"You did resort to a rather desperate measure," she teased.

He shook his head, grinning slightly. "That was unorthodox —not desperate. I was about to do far worse. Knock you over the head and drag you away. Keep you prisoner somewhere until I got it through your head that we were so right we had to be together. I might have even asked Susan to brew up a love potion."

Serena laughed. "But you don't believe in magic."

"No, but if I could get you to believe it existed . . ."

Serena slipped her arms around his neck and brought her body over his, loving the lift of his brow. She chuckled, wondering if she could ever be as happy again as she was at this moment.

"Oh, Justin," she murmured, "I love you so much I feel I might explode with it! And I've denied so much I've driven myself half-crazy. I still know nothing about you. I was jealous of Susan because she knew more about you than I did. I was even envying the Donnesys."

"We can solve that all easily enough." He laughed, cradling her body to shift it back into a curve next to his. He rose on an elbow to face her, running a tender finger along her shoulder and arm.

"Shoot," he murmured. "What do you want to know?"

"I . . . uh . . . I'm not sure!" Serena admitted, propping

her head upon an elbow too. "I just want to know about you. Anything and everything."

"Hmmmm . . ." he murmured playfully. "Well, my name is Justin O'Neill, no middle, and the doctorate is a Ph.D. I was born in New York City thirty-six years ago. I'm a Scorpio, which I understand is supposed to mean that you should beware of my sting. My parents were lower middle-class on the socioeconomic scale, but bright, wonderful people who believed highly in education. Both my degrees are from Columbia. I'm a teacher who likes to write on the side. I live right in Manhattan near the Museum of Modern Art. My hair and my teeth are still my own. What else?"

Serena laughed and impulsively pushed him back to his pillow, straddling over his waist to lean down and kiss him. "Who did you meet in Boston that night?" she demanded.

"A woman I've been sleeping with for about two years—hey!"

Serena had stiffened at his words and attempted to slide away from him, her eyes clouding over to him.

"Get back here!" he commanded gruffly, pulling her flat against himself. "I did have a life before I met you!"

"Yes, Justin," Serena protested, "but what a way to word a relationship!"

He shrugged, twining his fingers through the silky hair that floated over his shoulders. "The wording is correct, Serena. Oh, Denise is a nice enough person, and she can be witty and fun to be with. And she is very attractive—but she knows it and uses her every word and nuance. I'd hate to hear her give an honest explanation of her relationship with me. Her dream plan all along was to become first lady of the university."

Serena frowned slightly, lifting herself off his chest with splayed palms. "And you . . . you broke completely with Denise in Boston that night just because we met at the pond."

He smiled, liking the grind of hip against hip as she arched above him. "Yep," he said, lacing his fingers over the small of her back.

"Really?" Serena asked incredulously.

"Really."

She leaned against him once more, marveling at the comfort and ease of being together. They could love so tumultuously, then talk, enjoying the simple sensations of touching each other, finding their naked contact as natural as the night itself.

"Justin?" she murmured.

"Hmm?"

"Did you really have polio?"

"Yes."

"And that's why you became a health freak?"

"Health freak?" he repeated with chuckled resentment. "I don't run around eating alfalfa sprouts all day!"

Serena blushed, then ran a finger over his bicep, a muscle that was even immense in repose. "I mean the buildup," she mumbled.

"The buildup was mainly the polio, or consequences thereof. Even when I beat the disease, I was one of the scrawniest, rug-rattiest kids you'd ever want to see. And New York neighborhoods can be tough. I spent grammar school receiving black eyes; by high school I had my nose broken twice. And by then I'd had it, period. I simply decided that I wasn't ever going to lose a fight again."

"And did you?" she couldn't help inquiring.

"Nope. Not that I've been accosted by any street gangs lately." He stroked her hair at the base of her neck and said quietly, "My turn. Your husband really died jogging?"

Serena nodded. The thought was still a deep ache, but with Justin the ache was soothed.

"That doesn't make exercise bad, Serena. For most of us it's necessary for good health."

"I know," Serena whispered.

Justin abruptly changed the subject. "Tell me about your brother."

"Tom? He's an eccentric lamb!" Serena laughed. "He lives out on the Cape. He . . . we . . ." She suddenly took a deep breath and pulled away to sit on the bed, hugging her knees to her chest. "Our parents died within a year of each other due to

109

two freak accidents. My dad was electrocuted when a line went down while he was trying to make it home that winter the blizzards devastated the entire Northeast. My mom died the next winter; she was visiting a friend, and a small cargo plane crashed into the house. I had just graduated from high school and Tom had a year to go. Neither one of us was especially talented at anything, but we had the Golden Hawk, so we re-opened it as an inn. It was a rough time—until Bill, my husband, came along. He was driving through from Maine, and Tom met him in a restaurant in town and brought him home because he loved old houses. Tom had thought we might be forced to sell, but Bill fell in love with the place, and I fell in love with Bill." Serena paused for a second, biting her lip. She lifted her head with a proud tilt. "I was accused of marrying Bill for his money one day," she said with a touch of anxious bitterness, "but I didn't. He was simply the nicest, most caring man I had ever met."

Justin reached out to touch her chin. "I don't think anyone believes you married for money, Serena. I've heard it was a wonderful marriage."

She smiled her thanks hesitantly, then continued. "Anyway, Bill got Tom interested in real estate, so now Tom lives happily on the Cape making a fortune off his ventures every summer. He has places from Hyannisport to Provincetown. He zooms in here every so often, and I go out there now and then, usually in winter. Sounds like a silly time to go to the Cape, I know, but he has a motel in a little town called Dennis with the most beautiful indoor swimming pool you've ever seen. It's a marvelous feeling to watch the snow piled high outside while you're drifting in luxurious heat!"

Justin rose to sit Indian fashion and place his hands upon her shoulders. "I would just love to see the pool," he said, eyes brilliant with a soft, tenderly teasing light. "Think Tom could make arrangements for us to have it to ourselves? I'd love to be in the water with you, naked, feeling the heat of the water and you while watching the snow."

Serena half smiled, blushed slightly, and threw her arms

around his neck to hide the frightened pleasure in her eyes from him. Justin laughed; the force of her movement took him unawares, and they both tumbled backwards.

He lifted her easily and set her atop of his hips once more. "I know you're anxious for a good thing, witch," he teased, "but we have a few things to settle here first."

Serena arched a brow, then lowered her eyes.

"Marc," she murmured.

"You're going to talk to him first thing in the morning, Serena. It's only fair to him as well as us."

"I know," Serena murmured uncomfortably. "I—I will talk to him. As soon as I can. I'm not sure I'll see him in the morning."

"Don't wait, Serena," Justin warned, and she shivered a little at the tone of his voice. "I've had to watch him touch you since I've been here, and I can't guarantee you I'll stand around politely looking the other way anymore."

"I'll talk to him," Serena repeated, her tone a weak whisper.

He seemed to accept her words. He reached up to smooth her falling hair behind her ears. "There's one more thing I want to tell you tonight, Serena," he said, his voice so serious and intent that a shiver of fear suddenly raced through her.

"What?" she demanded thickly. They had talked, they had said they loved one another, and they had proven that incredible chemistry that bound them. But they had made no promises; no future had been assured. She was gripped by a paralyzing fear that he would tell her now that he would eventually leave her, that an obstacle still stood in their way.

"I have a daughter," he said.

"What?" she repeated, relief making her weak.

"I was married briefly in college. The marriage was a disaster, but I still consider Jenny my finest achievement in life. She's sixteen years old, exceptionally together for a teenager, and a joy to be with. I have custody for certain holidays and a month every summer. I want you to meet her."

Serena started to smile, and her smile slowly lit her eyes to the dazzling sapphire shade that so bewitched him. She bent

111

low and kissed his lips slowly and lingeringly, then raised her face just an inch above his.

"I'm going to love your daughter, Dr. O'Neill," she promised solemnly. Then she kissed him again, nibbling the circumference of his mouth before playing the tip of her tongue against his teeth. She pressed hard against him, taunting both of them as she subtly rubbed her breasts and hips along his chest and pelvis.

She was suddenly caught in his arms and swept beneath him. He smiled wickedly with a glitter of flame stretching across the green of the hazel in his eyes. "Salem," he informed her, "hath never had a witch such as thee, my love!"

They were the last truly coherent words either would speak again that night. In response to the taunt of her body, he made love to her again with a fierce passion that left no doubt to his possession of her—nor of the threads in which he was likewise bound. As night turned to dawn, Serena learned all the wonders of belonging to such a man. Light was casting a dim shadow over the centuries-old inn when she finally slept, physically spent and exhausted, but complete and fulfilled in a way she had never thought possible.

There were moments in the shadowland of wakening when she wondered if the events of the night had really been, or if she had dreamed again. She drifted, wanting to know that all was real . . . and then slowly assuring herself that it was so when she felt him, curled beside her, his arm cast casually around her. She stirred happily, edging even more closely against him, only to freeze when a furious tapping began at her door.

"Serena! You're oversleeping! You're going to run late. Serena!" The loud tapping started over until she bolted up in a wide-eyed sitting position.

"I'm awake, Martha, thanks! I'll be down in just a minute!"

She suddenly felt herself hauled back down to bed and imprisoned in a wonderfully strong pair of arms.

Justin kissed her, murmuring "Shhh" as she laughed, then tickling her so that she couldn't quiet her growing shrieks. He

112

released her as quickly as he had grabbed her, and sprang from bed, wandering about in search of something.

"What are you doing?" Serena whispered.

"I'm going to sneak out the back way," he told her dryly, pausing to glance seriously into her eyes. "It will be the last time, but I want you to have a chance to talk to Marc."

Serena lowered her eyes, knowing she was a coward, but dreading the confrontation nevertheless.

"Serena." Justin's enunciation of her name growled with warning.

"I will talk to him," she murmured unhappily. He had begun tearing apart the sheets again, and she demanded, "What are you doing?"

"I can't find my robe," he muttered.

Serena chuckled softly. "Does it matter? Who are you expecting to meet in a secret staircase?"

He glanced at her with dry reproach. "No one, I guess, but I still feel absurd sneaking around miniature chambers in the raw. Ahhh—found it!" He secured the robe around his frame and leaned across the bed to kiss her quickly. "Want to go into Boston tonight?"

She couldn't help lowering her eyes. "I—I won't see Marc until tonight."

He stiffened for a moment. "Want me to be there?"

God, no! Serena thought, it was all going to be bad enough to begin with.

"No, thank you," she tried to say calmly. Her voice finally steadied, and she added softly, "I owe Marc this much."

He shrugged, gave her a hard gaze, and sauntered over to the wall where he turned back to her for a moment. "I have to get into Boston myself, Serena, so I'll go ahead and do it tonight. A colleague is working on some tricky trial transcripts for me that show definite relationships between the accused girls during the witchcraft scare and a number of patients of Charcot." He paused for just a second after his explanation. "Serena, when I get back, I want things solved—or I'll take steps in solving them." He smiled a bit grimly to ease the words which were not threat but fact.

Serena smiled weakly in return.

He found the spring with little fumbling, and the panel slid silently aside.

A second later he had disappeared as if he had never been there.

Serena bit her lip nervously but then decided not to worry for the moment. She stretched her hand across the bed where he had lain, smiling as she felt the warmth. She wished that she could spend time just lying there, hugging the beauty of the night to herself in memory, but she was already late.

I wish I could go back to sleep, she thought more practically. But she couldn't go back to sleep either, so she forced herself out of bed and into a quick, cool bath. She didn't soak long, just giving herself enough time to be convinced she was awake. Then she hopped from the tub and dressed hurriedly, wincing occasionally as sore muscles reminded her that her night had been a wild one. But she loved that soreness.

Not even the brooding picture of Eleanora could dampen her mood as she scampered down the stairs. Poor lady, Serena thought with a gentle smile to the picture. Eleanora had been guilty of only one type of witchcraft—that of love.

In the kitchen Serena quickly poured herself a cup of coffee to gulp down. Martha came bustling in from the dining room as Serena stood drinking it.

"You aren't that late, Serena Loren," Martha chided. "You go sit down and eat a good breakfast."

"I am that late!" Serena pleaded, unable to suppress a yawn. Martha eyed her with critical inquiry, and Serena quickly added, "Okay, I'll take some bacon and toast on a paper plate—and I'll eat every bite, I promise!"

Martha gave in, and Serena hurried to her car with her breakfast in hand. As she eased her car down the driveway, she saw a flash of movement in the trees and smiled.

Justin was out jogging.

Her smile faded slowly as she wracked her mind for an explanation to give to Marc. She chewed hard on a piece of bacon, grinding the food with her teeth in an effort to concentrate. She finally gave up. There wasn't a decent explanation to give to Marc, and she couldn't worry about it until she absolutely had to because it was Saturday and the museum would be insane.

Susan took one look at her face and dug up some sympathy, offering to be the "witch guide" even though it was once more Serena's turn. Serena accepted gratefully, then discovered she was too agitated to stay behind the ticket booth controlling the crowds. After lunch she and Susan switched, and at least the hectic pace of the day made it speed by.

Serena had decided she would talk to Susan and try a rational explanation of all that had happened, and seek her usual, cool advice. With the last book sold and the tail end of the tourists filing out the door, Serena hurried to her office in black cloak and pointed hat and slid into the desk chair without bothering to discard her props. She wasn't sure if Marc would drop by the museum or simply appear at the inn. She wanted to quickly finish her daily bookkeeping so she would have a chance to talk to Susan.

She was tallying a row of receipts when she experienced a little prickle at the nape of her neck. Glancing up, she saw a woman hesitating in the doorway.

She was a stunning figure, dressed in an off-white form-fitting skirt and sophisticated bolero jacket and hat. Her hair was dark and confined without a single strand out of place beneath the contemporary dip of the chic suede hat.

"Serena Loren?" she inquired.

Serena nodded slowly, noticing that the woman's makeup was as perfect and suave as her dress. She was perhaps a year or two older than herself, and apparently perfectly assured.

"Can I help you?" Serena asked, instinctively cautious.

The woman entered and gracefully sat in the chair before the desk, posture stunningly erect as she calmly stripped off white gloves from elegant fingers. "Actually," the woman said dryly, "I've come to help you."

115

"Oh?" Serena lifted a brow and idly tapped the side of her chin with the eraser end of the pencil.

"Yes. My name is Denise Marshall. I'm an old friend of Dr. O'Neill's—a very old friend."

Serena stiffened but smiled politely. "How nice for you," she said nonchalantly, fully aware immediately that this was the woman Justin had been "sleeping with"—and also aware that she must appear absurd in her cloak and hat while Miss Marshall looked as if she should be modeling in the most elegant salon.

She was surprised that her comment had brought a slight flush of annoyance to the other woman's face.

"I don't think you quite understand, Mrs. Loren. That's why I'm here. I've just seen Dr. O'Neill in Boston."

Despite herself, Serena felt a stab of jealous fear and pain. She had to carefully force herself to continue to stare at Denise.

"Well, Miss Marshall," she murmured cordially, her trace of sarcasm so scant it might be doubted, "that's nice too."

The elegant hands folded and unfolded with agitation. "You really aren't understanding, Mrs. Loren, and so I'll get to the point. A week ago Justin informed me he had some absurd penchant for a woman he had seen only once—but that in fairness to me he thought we should break our relationship. Knowing Justin—boys will be boys—I allowed him his flight of fancy. He actually told me he was bewitched"—here Denise Marshall allowed her eyes to scan over Serena and flicker with amused contempt—"and I rather understand now what he meant. But I didn't leave Boston, Mrs. Loren, because as I've said, I know Justin. When I ran into him today at the Pru, he spoke of you again, so that's why I'm here." She paused for a moment, drawing a deep breath. "Mrs. Loren, you can be nothing but a passing fancy to Justin. I don't think you quite realize his position. We're not terribly big on . . . witches . . . in New York, and I seriously believe that even a short association with you could destroy his years of work within the university."

Serena was so stunned for a second that she couldn't think of a thing to say. Then she smiled. "Miss Marshall, I know this will come as a terrible shock to you, but I really think I know Justin far better than you do. And whether I do or not, I intend to give him a little faith. But just so that you don't worry, I will assure you I'll never wear my hat anywhere near his university."

"I'm trying to spare you from being hurt," Denise snapped. "He's not a marrying man, Mrs. Loren. If he does marry, he will only do so with a woman like me, one who can be the wife and hostess for his home. You see, we have an open relationship. Justin has had other infatuations. He's the type of man certain women don't stay away from—well, you obviously understand what I mean in that sense."

Serena felt a pounding in her pulse which was the beginning of a raw fury. She didn't want to lose her cool—nor bring herself to Miss Marshall's grasping-at-straws level. She took a deep breath, but before she could speak, Susan waltzed in—also in hat and cloak—and murmured an apologetic "Excuse me" with a sweet smile.

"Sorry to interrupt, Serena, but I simply can't find any bats' eyes, and we need them tonight."

Serena's fury dissipated as she bit her lip to keep from laughing at the look of sheer horror which replaced the composure in her unwelcome guest's eyes.

"We do have bats' eyes, Sue," she said with feigned impatience. "They're behind the left shelf with the wasp wings."

Denise Marshall stood, definitely looking nervous as she glanced from one sinister black-cloaked woman to the other. "I've given you fair warning," she murmured, backing out of the room.

Sue narrowed her eyes. "Is this—woman—threatening you, Serena?" Without an answer she spun on Denise's retreating figure, lifted her arms high so that the cloak swept out around her, and with eyes gone ridiculously wide, she began to chant something.

Denise turned and fled.

Serena and Sue both broke into gales of laughter. By the time

Serena could control herself, she had tears in her eyes. "What on earth were you chanting, Sue."

Susan started to chuckle again. "It was Latin—a spell to make the grass grow green."

Serena started laughing again, and then sobered abruptly. "Oh, Sue! What a mess I'm in!"

"Dr. O'Neill, I take it."

Serena nodded. "I need to talk to you, but I need to talk to Marc tonight, and I'm afraid he might walk in at any minute. Oh, Lord, he might have come across Miss Marshall! Damn, what a disaster!"

"Marc isn't going to walk in at any second," Sue assured her. "Martha called during the last tour to tell you that Justin had to drive into New York for the night and that Marc sailed by to drop off something for you and then said he wouldn't be back until the morning. The Donnesys and the Bakers are in Gloucester—so would you mind grabbing dinner out? That's the message, word for word or close to it."

"Oh," Serena murmured with a sigh. She had been given a temporary respite, and that made the night easier, but now she was back to dreading tomorrows.

And she also had to wonder how much of what the catty Miss Marshall said was truth.

"You're a fool if you fall for a single thing that woman said," Sue warned her. She hopped off the desk corner where she had perched. "Come on, you witch, you!" Sue laughed. "Let's go to dinner. I'm dying for all the juicy details—but I'm also dying for a juicy steak."

Serena cleared up the desk and followed behind Sue. Maybe this was just what she needed—a nice night out with a good friend.

But even as she was thinking that, she was also praying that Justin would come home and that he too would laugh when she told him about her encounter with the woman who claimed she could be his only spouse.

He would have to understand about Marc. What could she have done?

But more than anything, she wanted Justin to hurry home because now that she had had a night beside him, she knew that life itself was empty without him near.

CHAPTER SEVEN

Dinner with Susan was enjoyable. Hedging around the "juicy" parts, Serena told her friend about the events which had led to Denise Marshall's arrival.

"Honey," Susan said, brown eyes sparkling, "if I were you, I wouldn't worry about Marc, or about this Denise, or about anything else. Some things are just destiny, you know—fate! Damn!" Sue laughed. "I hope fate intends to be as kind to me!"

Serena smiled weakly, but her eyes were brooding as she idly chewed on her swizzle stick. "I am worried about Marc," she murmured. "And I am worried about Denise. Oh, not because she came in tonight like a tigress. But I mean, suppose she's right? What if I'm nothing more than a summer infatuation? I don't know how to explain it, Sue. I know that he loves me now —there is just something there—as if it's been there forever. But what if—"

"Serena," Susan interrupted. "The man obviously *isn't* hounding you simply to get you into bed—you've already been there. Honey, special things just don't come along that often. Go with it when they do!"

Serena quirked a brow. "Good vibes, huh?"

To her surprise, Susan hedged. "About Justin O'Neill—yes."

Serena frowned. "What do you mean?"

"I don't know," Susan murmured, draining her wineglass and lifting a hand toward their sunny waitress. "Something has been bothering me lately." She shrugged. "I don't like that picture."

"You mean Marc's painting of Eleanora?" Serena frowned again.

"Yeah, that's what I mean."

Serena's frown disappeared as she laughed. "Well, don't worry about the painting, Sue. I'm sure the first thing Marc is going to do after I talk to him is to defrock my wall!" She sighed. "I think I'll be glad to see the painting go myself."

The waitress arrived with the check, and Sue started to pick it up.

"Hand it over," Serena said.

"It's my turn," Sue protested.

"I'll write it off, tonight!" Serena laughed. "Business expense —we did work late! Besides, I can hardly expect the therapist to pay for the meal, can I?"

Sue shrugged. "Sometimes it pays to be the hired help." She linked an arm through Serena's as they left the restaurant. "I'll tell you, I'm sure not envying the boss tonight. You're right about one thing, Serena: reprieves are nice, but you should get it all over with Marc as soon as you can."

"First thing in the morning," Serena promised glumly, waving as they parted ways when they reached their cars in the parking lot. "Have a nice day off!" she called.

Sue waved in return. "Call me if you need me!"

As she drove home, Serena was torn between a desire to see Justin and a prayer that she wouldn't see him. When they were together, that feeling of everything being so positively right was with her. When she had time away, she was plagued by doubts about her own sanity. Logically, it was impossible to be so in love with a man she hardly knew. But she combated that logic with the "right" feeling. She hadn't known him long, but she felt as if she had known him a lifetime.

The parlor was silent as she entered the house, the lights dimmed. Pausing at the old-fashioned cherrywood phone desk,

Serena saw that Martha had left her a mile-long note. The Donnesys and Bakers were staying in Gloucester for the night. Dr. O'Neill had called to say he had found it necessary to drive into New York, but he would be back by late afternoon tomorrow. Marc had breezed back by and been very disappointed to discover Serena not home. He had left the book, and papers beneath the book, and he hoped Serena would enjoy his discovery as much as he had. "A real historical find." Marc would be there for breakfast. Serena should look at the book and papers.

Frowning, Serena bit her lip and crumpled up Martha's note. Why had Justin gone into New York? For a moment of petulance, she bitterly resented his ability to drive away. Then she sighed, reminding herself that she had gone into work this morning—he too had his responsibilities. Then she started to wonder if the chic and perfect Denise might also be heading back to New York.

"Stop!" she whispered aloud to herself, glancing down to the "discovery" Marc had left for her.

The book itself, she noticed, was encased carefully in a little black box with a plate of glass displaying an open page. Narrowing her eyes, Serena attempted to read a page. She felt a tiny shiver race up her spine as she saw the old script written across the pages. The writing was so different she could barely make out the words.

Marc had written his own note on top of the pages accompanying the book.

> "Serena!
> Believe it not, Eleanora Hawk's diary! Brought it to an expert to be transcribed, and then sealed for you. Found it when I tapped around the attic—was walled in just like Eleanora. Thought both diary and painting should be offered to the historical society—but they are both yours, love, you make the decision! Talk to you in the morning.
> Marc"

Serena winced at the note and then curiously glanced at the neatly typed pages that accompanied the book. She walked into the hallway to face the parlor—and stare into Eleanora's face. A chill seemed to sweep over her as she met her own eyes, glaring back as if they could see her.

"Dummy," she muttered to herself. Giving herself both a good mental and physical shake, she pulled her eyes from the picture, collected the papers and the book, and purposely started up the stairs. She laid her things on the bed while she took a quick bath, wishing that she would once more exit the tub to discover Justin in the room.

But her room was empty when she emerged in her towel, and she chided herself for foolishness as she slipped into a gown. Then she pulled down the covers of her bed and plumped up the pillows—and picked up the transcribed sheets of the diary, eyeing it a bit warily. But she didn't want to spend her night awake and tossing, worrying about Marc and missing Justin. And she had always loved the Golden Hawk. The inn had been in her family for countless generations. Both she and Tom had cherished their home and worked hard to preserve it. The legends had fascinated her since she had been a child, and she had never been afraid.

"And I don't want to be afraid of my own house!" she whispered aloud. "Marc and his damned ghosts . . ."

Be fair, she warned herself. Even Marc's pounding and tapping hadn't convinced her that ghosts abounded in her attic.

The only thing that had ever bothered her in the least had been the painting of Eleanora.

Don't be absurd; this diary is a real find.

She began to read the transcribed pages, grateful that Marc's "expert" had dispensed with the *thee's* and *thou's* that so often made historical reading tedious.

Minutes later she found her personal traumas fleeing her mind. The accounts by Eleanora were fascinating, and more than ever, Serena's heart went out to the young girl who had been forced into marriage with an older man she didn't love and then set to the task of obeying her Puritan god while becoming a virtual slave to the labor of running the inn. Hours ticked by while Serena read of the menial daily tasks that absorbed Eleanora's time. Life was, indeed, a hard lot. Serena began to skim the pages in an effort to learn more. Several entries caught her eye, and she reread them.

"I have not written in this journal for many days, for I have at last found a happiness. My son was born last Sabbath, and he is a bonny child, bringing me much joy. John too has left me alone since his birth, for lust is sinful. Men and women come together to procreate for the Lord, and I have pleased John with procreation. We have called our son 'David,' for it is a name of esteem from the Bible. . . ."

For page after page Eleanora wrote of her love for her son, and Serena bit into her lip without realizing it. Then another entry caught her eye.

"I do believe the town has gone mad. Little Ann Putnam from Salem Village has been taken with a strange illness; she has fits and cries out at all hours. They say her contortions are piteous to see, and my heart goes out to the child in her suffering. The doctor can find no cure for her, and he is crying out that it is the work of the devil."

Serena began reading the pages with a fever.

"May God in His goodness deliver us from this evil. They have hanged poor old Goody Nurse, and a better woman has yet to walk this earth. John Proctor speaks against the madmen in the streets, and now he too must stand trial. What demons do possess us? I have seen the afflicted girls in the courtroom; they are hideous in their pain. I know not what happens. Do witches walk freely among us? Surely not in the guise of such fine women as old Goody Nurse. . . ."

The next entry was several days later, and Serena felt as if her blood froze within her as she read.

"He came to me today, and God forgive me, for I can only believe that demons possessed me. I walked to the pond, having left David with the serving girl, and he was there. A more beautiful man I have never set eyes on before; he is built more sturdy than any ship, his eyes touch upon me like fire. I knew him not, but he touched me, and suddenly I was lost. Lust was sinful in his arms. . . .

"I know now who this Miles Grant is. He sails as captain on the *Pilgrim Queen*. He has come to the Golden Hawk to stay while his ship is refurbished. . . .

"I cannot stare upon him without a yearning in my heart. I would pray that God protect knowledge of my sin from my husband, but how may I pray to God when I have so deceived Him in my heart. . . .

"He came to my room tonight. He sought me out through the panels, and swore that he cared not should my husband slay him. I looked into his eyes and the brown that filtered the green was again like an anguished fire. I could not deny him. I have gone as mad as they who cry 'witch.' I love this man.

"He has taught me so much. Our love is not lust, nor is it sinful; it is natural, it is God's way that man and woman should love. He is so fine a person; he rails against the madness in the town, and through him, I have come to see so clearly. . . .

"I cannot live without him. Ours is a love that must last forever. I pray God shall not punish me too harshly in the next world, but if my love speaks the truth, then surely God will understand. I will go away with him, and I will pray that my husband will forgive me in this life, and that he may find happiness.

"This shall be my last entry in this ledger, for I must hide it, as I must hide myself. John Proctor and many others were hanged for witchcraft yesterday; the cries sweep stridently across the land, and now it is my name that they cry. My love is due to take me away, but he is at sea now. My good husband has forgiven me, and it is he who offers shelter now. None except the family know of the staircase; John will hide me when the jailors come to take me away. He will claim that I have left with a man, and then secret me out when my love returns. Blessed John. I weep with the pain I have caused him, I bless him with my every breath. . . ."

Serena's fingers were stiff and clammy, vised around the sheets. A coldness seeped over her, a terror which left her shivering as she reread the entries. . . .

"He came to me today. . . . I walked to the pond. . . . he is built more sturdy than any ship. . . . he came to my room. . . . the brown that filters through his eyes. . . ."

Serena threw the papers from herself and curled against the wall, trying to calm herself. "No!" she exclaimed aloud, then started taking deep, deep breaths.

She stood and began pacing the room. "I do not believe in . . . in what? Reincarnation? I don't! Coincidence, I believe in coincidence . . . and even coincidence isn't that strong. I'm a widow, not a poor adulteress seeking affection in the midst of a pathetic life. And Justin . . . is the farthest thing from a sea captain. . . ."

Despite all her logic, she was still shivering. "Why am I shaking? It is interesting, nothing more."

Serena closed her eyes for a second, then carefully picked up the book and the papers and set them on her dresser. I am going to go to sleep, she told herself, and tomorrow, I will read this with Justin, and we will laugh.

But when she was lying in bed with the covers drawn about her, she couldn't get her eyes to close. She kept remembering Eleanora's description of her lover's eyes.

"The hell with this!" she suddenly shouted aloud. She jumped from the bed and crept quietly downstairs to the liquor cabinet in the parlor and poured herself a double shot of whiskey, which she downed in a gulp, flinching as the liquor burned her throat. She closed her eyes with the sensation, then re-opened them to see Eleanora, staring down at her in the dim light.

Serena poured another double shot of whiskey. "Susan's right about you!" she told the painting. "Tomorrow—you go!"

With her hands finally steady, Serena started to close the whiskey bottle. She glanced at the painting again, then tucked the bottle under her arm. "Think I'm not going to sleep, eh? Well you're wrong! I am definitely going to sleep!"

In her room she had one more drink and finally began to laugh at her fears. It became easy to convince herself that they were unwarranted. The words in the diary began to fade as she ran her hand over the bed and the spot that had been Justin's last night. "I am so in love with him. . . ." she thought incredulously. The depth of that love and the beauty of it were still amazing.

She finally yawned and closed her eyes. She had much more pressing problems than a spooky feeling created by similarities in a diary to her own life. She would be seeing Marc in the morning, and then Justin would be back, and then she would have to start praying that her love and faith were justified, that the man she had given herself to so completely did love her with the inexplicable fervor with which she loved him.

She had a crippling headache in the morning. Getting out of bed was sheer torture, and hearing Marc's voice as she approached the dining room was agony on top of agony. She paused for a moment in the kitchen, taking a deep breath. This was it; she braced herself and moved through to the dining room.

"Good morning, Serena," Martha began, pouring her a cup of coffee. "You were out a little late—I do appreciate your not minding dinner out—so I didn't want to wake you." Although Serena was the one addressed, the last Martha said with an evil eye on Marc.

He stood from his seat at the table, laughing undaunted. "I

wanted to wake you, darling! What did you think? Isn't the diary incredible? Oh, Serena, do you realize what a find it is?"

Serena tried to smile. She picked up her coffee cup without sitting down. "Yes, Marc," she murmured, then took a long, stabilizing sip of the black coffee. "It's a wonderful find. It will surely make you famous in the annals of the state!"

"Not me, sweetheart—us!"

Serena swallowed more coffee with a wince. "Marc, take a walk with me outside, will you? I—we have to talk."

"Serena," Martha interrupted. "You should have something to eat first."

Oh, God, Serena thought, if I eat I'll throw up.

"I'm really not hungry," she said firmly. "Marc?"

A few seconds later they were walking beside the oak trees. Serena waited until they reached a little alcove with high, smooth-topped rocks. Then she sat and nervously stared at her fingers for several seconds.

"Serena—what is it?"

"I can't see you anymore, Marc," she blurted.

"What?"

"I—I'm breaking off with you, Marc."

"Why, Serena?" he stared at her, bewildered and obviously very hurt. Then he slammed his palm to his forehead. "I know, I've been neglecting you terribly—the book. Oh, honey, I'm sorry, I'll make it all up to you, I promise."

Tears started to fill her eyes, and she shook her head. "No, Marc, it's not the book. It's not you at all. It's me."

His tone changed. "I don't get it," he grated.

"Oh, Marc," Serena murmured miserably. "I'm sorry, really so sorry. I—there's really nothing to get—"

"I want to know why."

Serena lowered her eyes and swallowed. "I'm in love with another man, Marc."

"Who?" the demand was belligerent.

"Justin O'Neill."

"O'Neill!" Marc shouted incredulously. "I don't believe you! You barely know the man—"

"I do know him," Serena interrupted very quietly.

Suddenly Marc was kneeling before her, his eyes dark and earnest. "You may think you know him, honey, but you don't. It's impossible! Look, Serena, I can see where he interests you—he's like Einstein and Tarzan all rolled into one. But you can't trust a man like that, Serena. He probably has a girl in every state. He's probably been saying all kinds of things to you, Serena, but mark my words, honey, he's a man with one object in mind. You're a beautiful woman, Serena, and you're mature enough to know it. What he wants to do is get you in bed."

"Oh, Marc," Serena wailed, gritting her teeth with the frustration of making him understand. "I've already been in bed with him."

"What?"

He turned red with fury, and then white. And then his anger spewed from him. "You little bitch! You keep me at a ten-foot distance with your lily-white morality and then you hop into the sack with Mr. Virility without a qualm! O'Neill looked like a better time, eh?"

"No, Marc, you don't understand—"

"You're damned right, I don't understand, you . . ."

He proceeded to label her a number of names, each less complimentary than the other. For a second Serena sat white-faced, shrinking back from the abuse which she felt part her due. Then she could take no more.

"Marc—"

"Where, Serena, where?" At her refusal to answer, the anger in his features drew into a snarl. "While I was running around trusting you and believing you belonged on a pedestal, you were kissing me good-bye and jumping into his bed *in your own room!* A room you kept me out of. . . ."

He kept going. Serena had expected the reaction from him; she knew how hurt he was. But she hadn't expected his words to wound her as they were doing. Her headache compounded as he spoke. Each of the crude epithets he labeled upon her seemed in essence to be true. She had wanted to speak with him so rationally, to try to make Marc understand without bursting into tears which would appear ludicrous, but suddenly the tears were just streaming down her face. Guilt tore away at her. Justin . . . Marc . . . the diary. It was suddenly all too much. . . .

She stood, placing a hand before her as if she could ward off the lash of Marc's tongue.

"Stop it, Marc, please . . . stop it. . . ."

To her surprise, he went silent, staring at her.

"Serena?" She was chalk-white. He took a step toward her.

Inadvertently, Serena took a step backwards. Her foot hit the rock and she lost her balance and then stumbled against it, slamming the side of her face against it. Physical pain overrode that in her heart.

"Serena!" Marc was kneeling beside her, taking her into his arms, studying her face. "Oh, Jesus. Oh, Serena . . . I'm sorry . . . I'm so sorry . . . I didn't mean what I said, oh my God, look what you've done. . . ."

Her head was reeling, but she heard the tears in his voice. "It's . . . I'm okay, Marc." His concern suddenly hurt more than anything.

"You're not okay. . . ."

Well, she wasn't okay; the entire side of her head throbbed, and she could taste blood in her mouth, but what could she say to a spurned suitor who was crying beside her?

"It was all my fault—"

"It wasn't your fault!"

"We've got to get back to the house, honey—sorry, Serena. Your cheek is swelling terribly, and my God, I think you're going to have a black eye. We've got to get some ice. Maybe I should take you to the hospital. Oh, God, am I sorry. It's just that I was jealous of O'Neill from the first time I saw him, I guess. . . . I didn't mean to upset you, oh, God, you're hurt and it's my fault. . . ."

Marc kept trailing on, helping her to her feet, but suddenly she was struck with a fear more terrible than the haunting terror that had struck her last night.

O'Neill. Justin . . . he was due back any time. Dear God,

when Justin saw her face, he would be ready to commit murder. He knew she planned on talking to Marc, and he would never believe that what had happened had been an accident. And pitting Justin against Marc, it would be murder.

"Marc!" She exclaimed suddenly. "Please—do me a big favor. Just leave. I'll get some ice, I'll take care of myself, I promise."

Marc looked at her knowingly. "Serena, you're afraid that O'Neill is going to show up and think something worse happened. I'm not leaving. Not when you need help. I'll talk to him. I'm not a coward, Serena."

"Oh, Marc, I know that, but please! Marc, I want to let the entire thing become an incident that never happened. I'll—I'll drive out to the Cape for a day and see Tom. I want to see Tom, really, everything has been such a mess. . . . Oh, Marc, please, I very much want us to stay friends—I know what I'm doing, really."

"Oh, Serena, don't be so nice to me after the terrible things I said. This was my fault," he protested miserably.

"It wasn't your fault! I tripped. And God, Marc, I understand what you said . . . how you feel . . . the whole thing has been . . . unbelievable. But, please, Marc, forgive me, and let us all be friends. You're writing a book. You have to finish that book. We all *have* to be able to stay friends!"

"I can't run out when you're hurt—"

"Marc, please! Do it for me. I—I don't want to see Justin. I feel too terrible about everything. I want to see Tom. I'll be fine. Please, go!"

He stared at her with abject misery lacing his eyes, then leaned to gently touch her swollen cheek with his lips. "I'm going, Serena," he said quietly. Then he turned away from the alcove. Serena listened as his footsteps crunched through the trees.

Then she breathed a long sigh of relief and waited to hear his car start up. She was desperately longing for an aspirin. Between her self-induced hangover and the ringing in her head, she was beginning to wonder if she wouldn't rather be shot than anything else.

Finally she moved from the rock and slipped quietly across the lawn and into the house. Without realizing it, she studiously avoided the portrait of Eleanora as she silently trod her way up the stairs and into her own room, locking her door behind her. She gazed into the mirror above the dresser and drew back at what she saw.

The entire left side of her face appeared larger than the right. Dried blood drew a macabre line down her chin. As Marc had noted, the area around her eye was turning an ugly blue.

"Damn," she moaned, "how on earth did I manage that?"

She walked into the bathroom and took two aspirin and tried to bathe her face with a washcloth. Nothing was going to help. She would be lucky if the swelling went down by the morning. But at least by then she could think of some kind of excuse.

And she knew she had to have an excuse. There would be no way that Justin would believe what had really happened. She was so afraid he would act first and listen later, and the thought of Justin retaliating was more than chilling.

She was going to have to go to Tom's and *stay* a few days.

Susan would be ready to kill her, but Sue would just have to handle Monday and Tuesday by herself. "I'll be back by Wednesday morning, Sue, I promise!" she whispered, turning from her reflection. Back in her bedroom she threw a few things into an overnight bag. She hoped Tom hadn't planned a romantic weekend, because she was going to have to ruin it. It would be good for her to see her brother anyway. She could tell him all about Justin and see if he thought she had gone insane. And she could tell him about the diary, and he would make her laugh at the coincidences in life.

Justin was going to be furious to find her gone, but then he had stayed away a night, so he might as well learn it would be an equal partnership. He might want to strangle her, but it would be far better than his wanting to strangle Marc.

Serena opened the door to her room to shout her plans down

to Martha, then ducked back into the room in panic as she heard Justin's voice. Dear God, he was back ahead of schedule.

Serena leaned against her closed door and drew the bolt. Damn! Her gaze flew across the room to the panel, and she gripped her purse and bag and impulsively stuffed the diary and papers into the bag. Then she hit the panel with an experienced hand.

But she was carrying too much. In her attempt to reclose the panel, she jammed it. "Damn!" she muttered, throwing her weight against it. It slid into place, but she heard something snap. "How on earth did I ever let things become such a mess!" she moaned. She had forgotten a flashlight, and with the panel closed, she couldn't see a thing. "I'm going to have lights put in first thing I get back," she muttered, slipping her purse and bag over her shoulder so that she could feel the walls. She knew the steps well, so going down was not a tremendous difficulty.

Except that when she got to the bottom, the lower panel refused to give. Frowning, she set her paraphernalia down at her feet. Very carefully she ran her hands over the boards.

Something simply wasn't giving.

She was more puzzled than frightened at first; the staircase had been used by the family through the entire four centuries during which the house had stood. The original Hawk had built a sturdy home; Serena had repaired the roof, and plastered and painted, but the Golden Hawk had never needed much else. It was unthinkable to her that the panel shouldn't slide quietly as always.

Minutes later she was sweating profusely; the hands that stupidly continued to run over the boards were clammy. This is ridiculous, she thought. In a second it will give, I will be standing in the secret entry, and then I will be outside in the breeze.

But the panel didn't give.

A creeping chill of fear raced up Serena's spine, but she ignored it. She would just go back up to her bedroom.

But the memory of the snap she had heard stayed with her as she groped her way back up. And even as she touched the upper level paneling, she knew it wasn't going to give.

She sank down to the top step, feeling the darkness seem to sink into her. Don't panic, Serena, don't panic.

Be deliberate. Careful. Study the situation.

She turned and began pounding on the boards, until she tired herself into control.

"That," she mocked her sore hands aloud, "was not calm and deliberate. . . ."

Because I'm not calm.

I am calm. I am calm. Whispering the words, she tried the paneling again. And again. And again. And then walked down the steps to the first-level panel. And she tried there, again and again.

And then pitched her head back and screamed.

"Help! Oh, please help! Help! Help! Help!" She kept screaming until her voice went hoarse. Surely someone would realize soon that she wasn't around. They would start looking for her.

She leaned her head against the wood and slid to the floor. Wait, and then start screaming again.

But she wouldn't be heard. The insulation in the old house was as sturdy as its base. Eleanora must have screamed and screamed and screamed.

"Oh, my God!" Serena wailed. She leapt to her feet again and pounded against the boards and screamed at the same time.

This was it. Right here. This was where John Hawk had locked his adulterous young wife to die. Almost four hundred years ago another woman's screams had rent the air.

"*No!*" Serena shrieked, throwing her weight against the panel again. "*Noooo!!!*" Something seemed to snap within her just as surely as the paneling had done.

"I am not Eleanora Hawk, and I am not going to die in this stupid staircase! I am Serena, Serena Loren!"

But a voice seemed to mock her back. You are a Hawk; you were born a Hawk.

He came to me today.

As the darkness crouched around her and her screams died to leave only still, stagnant silence, she buried her face in her hands. "Oh, God." It felt as if the dark staircase embraced her tighter and tighter, as if the staircase had become a living malevolent force itself.

Eleanora had died here.

And now she was going to die again, perhaps so that her spirit could fly free.

"I'm not going to die," Serena whimpered aloud. "They will find me."

But as she sat there, the similarities became all too clear. The darkness preyed upon her mind.

He came to me today. He is built more sturdy than any ship. I went to the pond. . . . his eyes touch upon me like fire. . . . I could not deny him. . . . He has come to the Golden Hawk. . . .

The words repeated themselves over and over, louder and louder, until she clapped her hands to her ears, certain that she could hear the bitter shrieking laughter of Eleanora Hawk.

Serena slammed her weight against the paneling one more time. "Let me out! Let me out! Let me out! For God's sake, let me out!" Her screams became whimpers, her whimpers, sobs. And then the staircase was silent as she fell to the floor in a dead faint.

Things had gone badly since he left. The trip to Boston had been to track down papers belonging to Increase and Cotton Mather through a Professor Boswick. Boswick had cordially met him at the Prudential Building, only to shake his head and tell him the references he sought were in New York City, catalogued to a small, government library. He had said his thankyous and good-byes to the nice old professor and sat debating his next move. He needed the references, but he longed to be with Serena.

Serena had to talk to Marc.

And it was going to be a painful experience; she might be just as happy not to see him that night.

And then, while he had been deliberating between logic and libido, Denise had made an appearance.

He had tried to be polite, but when graciousness failed, he

135

had been brutally honest—deciding then and there that Serena would be having her own problems.

He escaped Denise quickly and called the Golden Hawk and headed back for New York. Through all his work, through the long, long night, he had realized more and more how deeply he loved her. He had known she was beautiful, he had known she compelled and enticed him as no other woman, but last night he had learned that they were irrevocably bound and she had become completely his. His streak of possessiveness was astounding, but it didn't matter because he was, in turn, possessed.

I love you, Serena, he thought as he lay alone, dreaming. I wonder if you can ever realize how deeply I love you.

In the middle of the night he got up and called his daughter. His ex-wife was less than thrilled with the phone call, but at his insistence, she had awakened their daughter.

"Jenny, I'm going to get married."

"Are you okay, Dad?" Jenny had asked softly. "I mean, you're not drunk or anything?"

"I resent that, young lady! No, I am not drunk. I have simply met the most wonderful . . . witch! I want you to come to the wedding."

"Dad! You're serious!"

"Of course I am."

"When?"

Justin thought for a minute. Then he smiled slowly. He hadn't exactly discussed any of it with Serena yet. "Next Saturday. Think you can make it?"

Jennifer laughed delightedly. "I can't believe it, Dad! I didn't believe anyone would ever snare you again! But of course. I wouldn't miss your wedding for the world. I'll call the airlines and arrange a flight first thing in the morning. Mom won't mind. She's going on some kind of a cruise."

He gave Jenny the number to the Golden Hawk. "Arrange your flight into Boston. I'll pick you up there."

And this morning, he had driven back like the wind. And now he felt wonderful—he would see her.

No one was in the hallway. He was so glad to be back that he smiled a greeting to Eleanora before calling a loud "Hello!"

Martha hurried in from the kitchen, drying her hands on a dish towel. "Dr. O'Neill! How was your trip?"

"Just fine, Martha, thanks. Where's Serena?" Justin wondered if he sounded as anxious as he felt.

"Oh, she must be out with Marc somewhere. That girl! Wouldn't eat a thing for breakfast. Just asked him to go for a walk with her. Then the car drives off, and she didn't say a thing to me." Martha frowned for a minute. "That's not like Serena," she added quietly. "Not like her at all. She's so responsible about letting me know what she's doing. But then she did look terribly drawn this morning."

"How long has she been gone?"

"Oh, not fifteen minutes."

Justin clenched his teeth against pent-up frustration. Maybe she hadn't seen Talbot last night—maybe this was the first chance she'd had to talk to him.

Maybe she had decided she wasn't in love. Maybe she was going to discover that she did care for Marc Talbot, the man she had known so much longer.

No! His nails dug into his callused palms. She was his, she was settling their future, and he was just going to have to wait.

"Won't you have some breakfast, Dr. O'Neill?"

"No, thanks, Martha."

He bolted up the stairs and reappeared a few minutes later in tank top, sneakers, and shorts.

If he had to wait, he was going to run. Work off some of the nervous tension gripping him.

Martha met him in the hall again. "I'll break the time rules and have some nice hot cakes when you get back." Martha's statement was really a query. "Maybe Serena will be back by then. It's not like her . . ."

"Sounds fine, Martha," Justin agreed, giving her a smile.

He stretched on the porch, then started running down the path. He kept his pace fast, and he kept running.

Every footstep was a heartbeat. Come back, Serena, I need you, I can't stand the waiting, I love you.

I believe in us.

I want to marry you.

I believe in . . . magic.

CHAPTER EIGHT

He ran six miles, bathed, and ate Martha's breakfast, and started getting really nervous. Where the hell was she? How could she be gone so long?

I have to trust her, he thought.

But then it wasn't a matter of trusting her; it had become a matter of worrying about Marc. He had always seemed a decent enough man, a little self-centered, but apparently with his basic values in the right place.

Justin tried to work, but realized immediately that the effort was ludicrous. He really couldn't give a damn about Cotton Mather, Ann Putnam, or even poor Giles Corey who had been pressed to death with his refusal to confess himself a witch.

By two thirty in the afternoon he could stand it no more. He pelted down the stairway and found Martha in the kitchen shelling peas.

"Martha, I'm a little worried about Serena. Have you got a phone number for Marc Talbot?"

If Martha thought it curious her guest should be worried about Serena when she was out with a man she had dated for a year, the lady showed no sign.

"There's a book right in the phone desk there in the hallway, Justin. Look under *T.*"

139

"Thanks," Justin murmured, trying to smile lightly as he realized he had now made Martha worried.

He had to dial twice to get the right digits. And then the phone rang and rang.

"Damn!"

He drummed his fingers on the cherrywood for a minute and then flipped through the address book for Susan's number. But Susan hadn't seen Serena either, and although Susan assured him that Marc was not in the least homicidal, Justin was aware when he finished the conversation that he had managed to make Susan worry too.

Justin sat at the desk and raked his fingers through his hair. I'm overreacting, he tried to tell himself. She had really only been gone a matter of hours.

He raced upstairs and changed back to a pair of shorts. "I'm going to the pond for a swim, Martha," he told the house-keeper, wondering why he had made the announcement. He came and went frequently without feeling it necessary to hand out his schedule.

He swam a number of strenuous laps, panted on the shore-line, indulging in a frenzy of push-ups, and then swam again. He stared at the sun, wondering if it had really allowed time to pass when his mind would simply refuse to let it do so.

He grabbed his towel and walked back to the inn.

Martha was waiting for him at the door, her brows furrowed in worry. "Justin, Marc just called—for you. He sounded rather anxious when I told him we both thought Serena was with him. Call him right back, won't you?"

Justin was on the phone in seconds, heedless that he dripped over the glossy, polished wood floor.

"O'Neill?" Marc inquired.

"Yeah," Justin replied. His fingers trembled around the re-ceiver. "Where's Serena?"

"Listen, O'Neill, I called first because I felt I had to explain Serena's reason for leaving, except that I'm worried sick now myself. She had told me she was going to drive out to Tom's,

140

but Martha says her car is still there and that she hasn't seen her since she left with me."

A pounding began in Justin's head. "Why was she going to go to her brother's?"

Marc hesitated over the wire. "She tried to tell me it was because she was upset and simply wanted to see him. But that wasn't the reason. We, uh, we had an awful argument. And she was upset. So upset that she tripped and fell . . . and wound up with a scratched cheek and the nice beginnings for a black eye—"

"What?"

"She was trying to get rid of me, O'Neill. I guess she had decided you might not have believed what really happened, and she was so upset that I . . . I did as she asked."

Justin felt his blood beginning to boil. "She was hurt because you fought with her and then you left her—"

"She was afraid for me, O'Neill," Marc said bitterly. "And listen, I'm still trying to comprehend the fact that she's in love with you." Marc's voice was quiet. "I've been in love with her for a long time, Doctor."

Justin clenched his jaw and held his temper, sighing. Dear God, did she have that little faith in me? But then maybe she had been right. If he had seen her hurt, after she had been with Marc . . .

"Don't you understand? Serena felt she had to make me leave, and then leave herself, because she wanted us all to be able to be friends," Marc continued. "But I couldn't leave things at that. I didn't think you'd understand *her* leaving like that . . . and, well, I don't like what's happened . . . but she's in love with you and I can't change it and I said such terrible things . . . I had to call and tell you the truth before you started thinking something much worse because it appeared as if she had just walked out . . . that wasn't it. She was afraid you'd kill me."

Oh, God, Justin thought with a groan, aware that Marc spoke to him with fear and a definite, unexpected integrity.

"Listen, Talbot, I have no desire to kill you. I wish Serena

141

would have had a little faith . . . none of that is important at the moment. I'm worried about a whole lot more than an argument between the two of you and a possible black eye. Get out here—maybe you can think of something. I'm going to try her brother."

"Be right there," Marc replied solemnly.

Justin dug through the book for Thomas Hawk. He was able to reach only a switchboard operator who informed him Mr. Hawk was gone for the day.

Setting the receiver down, Justin saw that Martha hovered nervously behind him in the hallway, wringing her flower-patterned apron with plum-gnarled fingers. He forced himself to smile and softly suggest, "Could you put on a pot of coffee, Martha? I could really use a good cup of coffee. And a sandwich. Would you mind?"

Martha shook her head, her dark eyes wide and nervous, her gray hair looking quite frazzled. "Coffee, yes, Dr. O'Neill, it sounds like a good idea. I'll get right to it."

She left the hallway. Justin picked up the phone again and called the police, only to be informed that he couldn't even file a missing persons report this soon.

"The lady is an adult," the sheriff said, his voice irritating with official patronization. "If there was some kind of a little lovers' tiff, well, sir, she probably just wants a little time alone."

Justin didn't reply. He set the receiver down so hard that the desk chipped beneath it.

Something suddenly alerted him to a presence behind him. He turned to see a man standing just inside the doorway.

"Who the hell are you?" Justin demanded, fear and annoyance making the words a growl.

The young stranger lifted sandy brows and walked closer to glare at Justin with rather incredulous, sky-blue eyes.

"I might ask you the same thing," he replied dryly. "I'm Thomas Hawk, coowner of the inn. Who are you?"

He was a lot like his sister; his eyes were the same startling shade, registering both intelligence and wit. He lit a cigarette

142

and puffed it nervously while he listened to Justin. Martha returned from the kitchen, hugged him profusely, then left the men alone in the parlor with sandwiches and coffee.

"It's a surprise to see you now, Tom," Justin said, munching a sandwich without tasting it, "but a damned good surprise. I'm worried as hell, and the police think I'm a crank idiot."

Tom took a sip of coffee, and a slight blush colored his cheeks. "I don't suppose this will make much sense to you, O'Neill—you being a psychologist with a doctorate and all— but I, uh, came out today because I was worried about my sister. We . . . we can kind of tune in on each other sometimes. I've been thinking more and more about her the last few days, and this morning . . . well, I just had an urge—a compulsion—to come out and see if she's all right."

Marc suddenly burst in from the entryway. His eyes immediately lit upon Tom Hawk. "Tom, you're here! Did Serena call you?"

Tom shook his head. Justin rose and stared across the room at Marc. "Have you got any ideas, any at all, of where she might have gone? Think, Marc, some place like the pond, anyplace she goes—"

"She's in the house somewhere."

Both Justin and Marc turned to stare at Tom.

He looked back at them both. "I'm telling you, I know. She's in the house somewhere. Has anyone checked her room?"

It might have been a comedy of errors. They were like skyrockets—all three men taking a second to stare at one another stupidly, then bolting for the stairway. They crashed together at the landing, then Tom preceded Justin who preceded Marc.

"Serena?" Tom Hawk tapped at his sister's door, then hearing nothing, tried the knob.

"Bolted," he murmured.

"What?" Justin demanded incredulously. He stared at the door for a second. "Then she has to be in there—"

"I'll get the extra key from Martha—" Marc offered, but Justin hadn't heard him. A panic had welled within deeper than anything he had ever known. He charged his shoulder against the door. The wood buckled and splintered. He stepped back and plowed his frame against it a second time. The splintering wood gave, and the broken door groaned, hinges screeching, as it slammed to the floor. The three men bolted into the room, calling her name. Marc walked into the bathroom, then reappeared to shake his head in response to anxious eyes.

"But she has to be in here. . . ." Marc began, then fell silent. Justin was watching Tom Hawk, who had closed his eyes. They reopened. "The staircase," he said quietly.

Justin rushed across the room. He ran his fingers down the paneling, but apparently the old lever and spring had jammed. He backed up a few paces and rammed the wood. It groaned but didn't budge.

"Wait," Tom murmured, "that stuff is reinforced and insulated. It's a good foot thick—"

Justin glanced at him with glazed eyes, then glanced back at the paneling. He threw his body against it again and again. Tom and Marc both attempted to help, realizing from Justin's glance that to get help would take time.

The wood finally began to splinter. Panting, Justin halted the others for a moment and gave himself a ten-foot runway. He hurtled his body against the paneling like a catapult.

The old wood crackled in something like a death groan and shattered; Justin found himself sprawled out on the landing and then hurtled down several steps without standing. There was something sticky on his head which had to be blood. His shoulder felt as if it were being stabbed by a thousand pins.

"O'Neill, you okay?"

Justin shielded his eyes with a hand as Tom shot the ray of a massive flashlight down into the darkness.

"Yeah, I'm fine," he muttered, checking for broken bones as he struggled to stand in the confinement of the stairwell. "Get down here with that thing, will you?"

As Tom followed with the light, Justin carefully wedged his way down the steps. The light above shone on a bundle at the foot of the stairs, sunk against the wall.

"She's here!" Justin called out hoarsely. He raced down the remaining stairs and slid on the last, but he was right, Serena was there. She felt terribly cold to his touch; his probing fingers could barely find a pulse.

He scooped her into his arms and started to swear as he realized the second panel too was jammed. He turned and started back up the stairs with his limp bundle in his arms.

"Christ!" Tom Hawk muttered as he saw his sister. Justin laid her out on the bed and raced into the bathroom for a cold cloth. "Get Martha," he said as he began to bathe her face. Her lip was puffed and an angry blue bruise was spreading beneath her left eye, but Justin worried more about her color. She was shockingly white. He glanced at her hands and choked back a cry of pity; the palms and fingertips were raw and bloody from her pounding against the panels.

Martha, commendably calm, walked into the bedroom with a brandy bottle. She sat next to Serena and forced a sip between her lips. Serena coughed and swallowed. A more natural glow of pink slowly began to spread across her cheeks. Martha gripped her wrist and smiled to the three anxious men who hovered above her. "Pulse is strong now, poor little thing; she just must have scared herself half to death."

Tom Hawk avoided Justin's eyes. She should have been scared, he thought; no one can hear a thing from that stairway.

Justin came around the bed and slipped his arms around Serena, bringing her head to rest against his shoulder. He grabbed the cloth and bathed her face again, then motioned to Martha for the brandy. He managed to get her to accept another sip.

Her eyes began to flicker. And then they opened.

And stared into his, the sapphire pools seeming to grow larger every second.

And then she screamed, a bloodcurdling cry that echoed and riveted and echoed again around the room.

"Serena!" Justin attempted to soothe her, but she was fighting him madly. "Serena, it's me."

145

"Don't touch me!" she shrieked. "Don't touch me! Don't you ever touch me again, Miles Grant!"

Justin froze in pain and disbelief. Her eyes were brilliant with wild desperation; she continued to beat against him, nails clawing, arms and legs flailing—until she suddenly went limp again, her beautiful sapphire eyes closed.

Justin carefully placed her frame back onto the bedding. Then he stood and left the room, his face a mask of bewildered agony.

Sensations came to Serena before she opened her eyes. Her head felt very cool, and there was light; she knew it because the oppressive blackness was no longer with her.

The light actually hurt for a moment as her lashes lifted, and she tried to focus her vision. She reclosed her eyes immediately with gratitude. She was in her own bedroom, and her bed felt delicious. And not far from the bed, Tom was sitting cross-legged in a chair, munching on an apple and reading.

She opened her eyes a second time to find her brother watching her. "Hi," he said, leaving the chair to sit beside her on the bed and pick up her hand. "How're you doing?"

Serena smiled and nodded to his anxious inquiry. "Fine," she murmured. "Really fine." She hesitated a minute. "Oh, Tom, I'm so glad you . . . that you knew . . . that . . ."

"Ssh . . ." he murmured, exchanging a special glance. "They would have found you anyway, Serena. Your Dr. O'Neill had already called the police by the time I got here."

Serena frowned, unable to stop her bottom lip from trembling. "Oh, Tom. . . ."

Tom frowned in return. "What is it, Serena?" He paused a second. "O'Neill tore down half the house to get to you, Serena, and then you screamed your head off at him. Do you remember?"

Serena began to tear at the bedclothes with her fingers, not looking at her brother. "I'm scared, Tom," she said, her voice barely a whisper. She finally looked at him. "Have you seen the painting in the parlor? Marc found it; it's Eleanora Hawk."

Tom lifted a sandy brow and bit into his apple. "So?"

"Tom, that picture could be me."

Tom shook his head in confusion. "I wouldn't quite say that, Serena. There are similarities, but that really isn't a great shock. We are Hawks."

"Yes, but there's more, Tom. Marc found a diary—"

"Yeah, I know," Tom interrupted, rising to throw his apple core into the trash and walk back to her with his hands stuffed in his jeans pockets. "I've been reading it while I was sitting here. What a great find!"

"Yeah, a great find," Serena muttered bitterly.

"Serena." Tom sat again and took both her hands. "I realize that finding yourself caught in that stairway must have been terrifying. We should have ripped those damn panels out long ago. But I can't believe you're getting all upset because of the painting and the experience! You have too level a head for all that rot!"

Serena chewed furiously at her lip. "It's not just the painting . . . or even the stairway . . . I mean, oh, God—I was terrified! I don't remember shrieking at Justin, but I was so scared. . . ." Her voice died away as Tom anxiously clutched her hands, worried sick to see his so-reasonable sister such an unreasonable wreck. She wet her lips, not looking directly at him, and asked, "How far have you gotten into that diary, Tom?"

"Skimming—all the way through."

Serena kept chewing studiously at her lip. "How much have Justin and Marc said to you?"

"Not a lot," Tom said, laughing, "but enough for me to get the picture. You've broken off with Marc, and it's damned obvious that Justin O'Neill is madly in love with you. And you know, Serena—not that you need my approval—I think he's more the man for you than Marc. You're too independent for Marc, and he's not quite as secure a man as you need. You just might have found the real thing, sis."

Serena shook her head miserably. "Tom, you still don't understand. Didn't you read those descriptions of Miles? Damn, Tom, someone might have looked straight at Justin to have written those things! The eyes, Tom—"

147

"Actually, Serena," Tom interrupted with dry humor, "I haven't had a chance to stare deeply into Dr. O'Neill's eyes as of yet. But if they are hazel, so what? I would assume a good sixth of humanity—alive and dead—have, or have had, hazel eyes."

Serena shook her head again. "Oh, Tom—it's worse than that." She colored slightly. "Tom—I met Justin at the pond. And I—I—"

Tom stared at her curiously, knowing exactly what she was hedging around saying, and finding it hard to believe. He had been overly protective as a younger brother, but it had never really mattered. Serena had fallen in love with her husband, and that had been it. She had barely dated otherwise, and as a brother, he had often found Marc's frustration amusing.

And now she had met and made love to a man at a pond.

"Serena, if I hadn't discovered already that I like O'Neill, I'd probably want to bash his face. I'm glad I like him—'cause chances are good I wouldn't have a face left if he bashed back! But, words of wisdom from a younger brother. You must be as much in love with him as he is with you. There's nothing spooky about that, Serena, just wonderful."

"Oh, Tom, I don't know! Everything seems to be following a pattern. I met him at the pond. Then he came . . . here. Through the stairway. And I was so crazy in love, Tom. And then I wind up in the stairway! After four hundred years, two panels break! I can't help feeling that . . . that . . . something is strange—"

"Serena! You can't possibly believe in—"

"Tom, how can you, of all people, say that? Tom, I thought you would surely be the one to understand me! Okay, it's not like 'think black' and we know the color, but we do know things about each other."

"It's a form of ESP, Serena," Tom said softly. "A mind science, one not completely understood, but they have millions and millions of things left to be discovered about the complexities of the mind! That's different than avenging ghosts or reincarnation or things that go bump in the night."

Serena searched her brother's eyes and then sighed. "I know all that, Tom—"

"And you came out of the stairwell safely."

"I know that, too, Tom. But what about Justin? What if something happens to him because of me?"

Tom stood and smiled at her. "You'd better discuss that with Justin. He's been pacing the floor downstairs for two hours now. If I don't stop him, he'll wear through boards that have withstood centuries!" He paused a second. "Can I send him up?"

Serena touched her face nervously and then nodded. Tom paused only another second to ruffle her hair. "You sure you're okay? We thought about calling a doctor, but Martha said there was no real damage."

Serena tried to smile with assurance. "Yes, I'm really okay, Tom. And . . . I do want to see Justin . . . if just to talk. . . ."

Tom found Justin in the kitchen, staring blankly out the window as a cup of coffee grew cold in his hands. The intense hazel eyes immediately riveted to his.

"She's okay," Tom assured him quickly, pulling up a chair across from Justin at the small kitchen table. He hesitated a moment. "She wants to see you, but I think you should know a few things first."

Justin raised his brows.

"It's that damned picture, I think!" Tom exploded. "And then Marc found an old diary—Eleanora's diary. He was trying to do something special for Serena, and he had it transcribed and left it for her to read. It seems everything that has gone on between the two of you kind of happened before. And then Serena wound up in the staircase."

"Oh, Christ," Justin muttered, "Like Eleanora Hawk? Is that what you mean?"

Tom nodded.

"And that's why she shouted." It wasn't a question. Justin

sat lost in thought for a moment and then looked back to Tom. "Is she over it all now?"

Tom winced. "Yes—and no. She's still scared of something. I tried to reason with her. It's just that . . . well, dammit, O'Neill, you do fit the bill for Captain Miles Grant. And"—Tom paused to clear his throat—"hell, O'Neill, you have to read the damn diary. They, uh—Eleanora and Miles, I mean—they met at the pond. And Miles found the way to her room through the staircase."

Justin stared at Tom with disbelief. "You can't possibly believe that . . . that . . ."

"That Miles and Eleanora have come back?" Tom queried. "No, I guess I don't really. But I'm sure you've heard the story; they both met with disastrous ends."

Justin stood. "Thanks, Tom. I'm going to marry your sister next weekend. Think you can be here?"

A slow grin filtered through Tom's cheeks. "Sure," he said.

Justin began to walk out of the room. "Hey, Justin," Tom called. Justin paused. "I think you ought to get Serena out of here for a while. You're welcome out at the Cape."

Justin deliberated Tom's words. "Yeah, I think you're right. But I think we'll head into New York this time. And for tonight"—he paused, a tic pulsing in the thick cords of his neck—"I think we'll get her up and out. Why don't you find Martha and see if she wants to go to dinner? I'll talk to the Donnesys and Bakers quickly before I go up to Serena."

Justin wanted his plans set before he spoke to Serena. He hadn't been able to believe the way she had repulsed him; her screams had been daggers that dug into his flesh. And now he understood.

But he couldn't allow her to forfeit their love, their lifetimes, on a distant tragedy, no matter what the coincidences.

The elderly couples had returned while Tom was in with his sister, and Justin had explained only that Serena had locked herself into the stairwell. Now he went to the Donnesys and spoke with them quickly, asking for their help in anticipation of Serena's protests.

He explained his plan and received their enthusiastic response. Only then did he tap on the remnants of Serena's door, opening without waiting for her acknowledgment.

She was still lying in bed, exceptionally beautiful to him as she clutched the sheets about her. Martha had changed her into a long white gown, and her hair looked exactly like polished copper against the white. Her eyes were still huge and violet against the pale ivory of her face.

"Hi," he said.

"Hi," she returned.

Justin walked over and sat beside her on the bed.

"I love you," he whispered.

She burst into tears.

He held her, and she didn't fight him. He kept soothing the hair from her forehead, and finally she calmed down enough to talk. "Oh, Justin, I love you! But I . . . we can't be, Justin! Something terrible will happen. Oh, I know you think that I'm crazy, but I'm really frightened."

"Shh . . . Serena," Justin murmured. "Serena, there are similarities, but there are differences, too! I'm the farthest thing in the world from a sea captain. I have to inhale Dramamine for a week to get into a row boat! And you're a widow, sweetheart, not a philandering wife!"

"But, Justin—"

"I don't believe in reincarnation, Serena. Nor spirits of the past coming out in vengeance."

Serena stared at him, wishing desperately that she could be so sure. "Justin, you don't believe in things, but my brother came here today because he sensed, he knew something was wrong. How can you deny that?"

"I don't deny it. I fully believe that ESP exists. It's a new science, sweetheart, being studied more thoroughly all the time. But what you're afraid of is different, Serena."

Serena suddenly reached out and touched his chin, thinking how terribly much she loved him. She liked the feel of his slightly scratchy skin beneath her fingertips. She liked his face, the eyes so full of both humor and intensity. She loved the white teeth against the full-shaped lips and rugged bronze flesh.

And I could make something terrible happen to him.

"We're getting married next Saturday," he announced.

For a moment she forgot her fears. "What?"

"I think I'm going to have to buy you a hearing aid early," he teased. "I said we're getting married next Saturday."

"But . . . but . . . I thought you didn't believe in marriage."

He grinned. "I guess I do. Serena, I love you. I can't stand being without you. Want to tell me a nice yes?"

She discovered that she was able to laugh. "I didn't realize you needed my agreement. It sounded like an announcement."

"Yeah, I guess it did. An old mind trick, Serena. If I say something with authority, there's less chance you'll say no."

The laughter she had been feeling died away. She slipped her arms around his neck and pressed tightly, desperately against him. "Oh, Justin, don't you see? I'm afraid for you! I was locked in the stairwell. Now . . . now something awful could happen to you—"

"Serena, you were locked in the stairwell, yes, but you're out! And you're fine! The past is not repeating itself!"

She was shivering as he held her. He drew away to smile at her. "And you look gorgeous except for that black eye."

Serena glanced down nervously. "Where's Marc?"

Justin laughed. "Marc has gone home, and he's just fine, too. Lots of faith you had in me, young lady."

"I'm sorry," Serena murmured.

"Don't be," Justin admitted dryly. "If we all hadn't been so worried about you, I might have been tempted. But he's a nice guy, Serena. We can all be on good terms. He left now because he does still love you. It will take a little time for us all to be able to sit around a fire and chat."

Justin rose and reached out a hand. Serena looked at him doubtfully.

"Up, my love. Put on something nice. We're going out to dinner."

"Tonight?"

"Yep. You've had a nice long sleep, and there's not a thing really wrong with you. You're not going to sit around here and brood all night. Martha is already getting dressed up, and Tom is all set. Mildred and Gayle both said they'd be happy as larks prowling about the kitchen themselves. And then when we get home tonight, we're going to pack."

"Pack?" Serena repeated incredulously.

"Ummm. We're going to drive back to New York for a few days. I still have some research to do on home turf."

"But, Justin," Serena protested, "I can't leave! I have to open the museum tomorrow. Susan can't possibly handle the summer crowds alone!"

"Susan isn't going to handle them alone. She's going to have all kinds of help. Mildred and Gayle and Giles and Pierce."

"Oh, no," Serena murmured. "I can't . . . I mean, they can't . . ."

"And why not?"

As if on cue, the battered door that no longer really closed opened and in breezed Mildred Donnesy, who stared at Serena with her silver-blue eyes indignant. "If I can take over the entire world, Serena Loren, I can certainly help manage a little witchcraft museum for a few days!"

"It's not fair to you—"

"Posh! It will be sheer pleasure to really function as an indispensable commodity!"

Justin grinned at Mildred, then at Serena. "You're outnumbered, my love."

Serena glanced at Justin and heard the door quietly semiclose —this time, with a click. Mildred had left them alone.

She was still uneasy, still frightened.

But still so terribly, terribly in love with the man taking over her life. She noticed suddenly that a long jagged cut lay beneath a lock of hair on his forehead.

"Justin!" she exclaimed. "What did you do?"

He laughed. "Had a fight with the paneling instead of Marc!

That's okay. When we go out together, any busybodies can discuss us all they like. We'll look like battling marrieds!"

"Justin!" Serena protested with a chuckle. "Do you think we will be battling marrieds?" she asked.

"Only now and then." He reached down and kissed her, slowly and leisurely, reminding them both of the fires that could race through their blood.

He straightened. "I'm getting out of here," he said huskily, hazel eyes glinting like those of a demon, "or we'll never get to dinner. I'd help you dress, but I'm afraid I'd stop when I got the nightgown off!" He strode to the door, turned and smiled, and whispered a quick "Hurry," and then left, closing the fragment of her door behind him.

Serena watched him leave, thinking again how terribly much she loved him.

And how terribly—no matter how ridiculously—scared she was.

"New York," she whispered to herself.

It would all be all right in New York.

Or would it?

CHAPTER NINE

If anything was the opposite of the Golden Hawk, Justin's New York apartment was it.

The kitchen was small. A sparkling tile counter overlooked a large, long living space, and four leather bar stools were lined up in front of the counter. There was a contemporary dining set with an almost Oriental flair before the long room sank down a step.

A copper fireplace sat in the middle of the sunken area, flanked by chairs and a low couch in a cream-colored leather. The carpeting was a shade darker than the chairs, but the over-all lightness was offset by warm wood end tables and the inter-woven cream and brown drapes. The apartment really wouldn't have "looked" like Justin at all, except that the end tables and hanging glass shelves were covered with books and interesting little carvings, proof of his delving into the voodoo mysticism of the islands and the occultism of other places and peoples.

Justin watched her as Serena wandered into the apartment, smiling. She paused to examine a little leather satchel that hung on the wall, and he followed behind her, taking the item from its little hook and opening it for her.

"That's the medicine or magic pouch of a Shoshoni shaman,"

he told her. Then he laughed. "The American Indians had some rituals that would make even Sue's hair stand on end."

Serena laughed with him. Here, in New York, it was easy to forget she had been frightened.

"What do you think of the apartment?" he asked.

Serena replaced the satchel on the wall and slipped her arms around his neck. "I love it," she replied, brushing his lips with hers.

He grinned wickedly. "You haven't seen anything yet. Come on, I'll show you the balcony first."

It was more of a porch than a balcony. There was an area of concrete flooring with wrought iron chairs and a glass-top table, a profusion of hanging plants, and a gas barbecue grill. The concrete flooring ended to the left, and another set of hanging plants sheltered an area of raised wooden decking.

Serena lifted a brow to Justin.

"Whirlpool." He chuckled. "What else?"

He smiled. "My students are all at the grad level—nice, adult people." He took her hand and led her up the steps to the whirlpool, then past the whirlpool to another set of sliding doors. "Let me guess," Serena murmured. "Your bedroom."

"Our bedroom," he corrected.

Serena smiled and moved through the doors.

The bed, low to the floor, was the dominant fixture of the room. Its cover was a huge cowhide; it was backed by a low headboard of shelves and crannies. As in the living room, the sleek stylings of the headboard and dressers had a very contemporary, slightly Oriental flair. "Very nice, Dr. O'Neill," she murmured.

He chuckled. "I'm not really much on design myself," he admitted. "I never had time. The place was done by a decorator."

"Oh." She suddenly felt shy with him, realizing how much she still had to learn about the man she had agreed to marry in a week. An open door led back to the living room. She walked through it quickly and discovered two more doors off the long living area. She glanced at Justin as he followed her, and he

156

opened the first. "Guest bath, and"—he continued on to the second—"all the stuff to keep my ego going," he teased as he opened the second to display a room full of weights and other exercise paraphernalia.

Serena merely pursed her lips together with a half smile.

He came to her and pulled her into his arms, stroking her hair as she lay against his chest. "Not tremendous, but it will do for a while, don't you think?"

Serena broke away from him with a worried little frown. "Justin, don't you think we may be behaving a bit rashly. I mean, we haven't discussed anything at all. You're taking it for granted that I can just move to New York. What about the Golden Hawk? What about the museum? I've been working a long time, Justin. I put a lot into building up that museum."

He paused, silent for a minute, a wary shield over his eyes. "I'm a department chairman, Serena," he said finally. "I can't simply walk out of my job without notice."

Serena began wandering about the living room, picking up the little carvings in pretend study. Her heart was hammering as she wondered why she was trying to pick an argument. I'm not, she thought. These are things that have to be discussed.

"I *own* the Museum of Fact and Fantasy," she said, "but you expect me to just walk out."

"Don't be absurd," Justin interrupted impatiently. "I know we're going to have to make arrangements for management and all that, but I don't really see the problem. Sue can carry the place; we'll have to hire an assistant for her. I'm sure she'll know someone capable, maybe another witch from her coven."

"There's the Golden Hawk—"

"Where Martha already does all the work."

Serena spun around. "But what about me, Justin? I'm not Denise. I can't spend my life being a faculty wife!"

The hazel in his eyes darkened; Serena saw the tightening of the muscles in his face. Her heart fluttered for a moment as she also saw the stretching of his cotton shirt across his frame. It was so easy to read Justin's anger: the slightest inward twitch of annoyance became visible because his physique was so well toned.

"Serena, you're picking at things because you're still scared. We have lots of time to decide on the future. Maybe we won't stay in New York; maybe we will make Salem our home. Maybe we'll decide to move to Nevada, who the hell can say? But right now, we're staying away from the Golden Hawk and all that absurd mumbo jumbo about Eleanora and Miles! Do you understand?"

Tears started to prick her eyes as she realized he was right; she hadn't left her fears behind her at all. They were inside of her, as deep-seated as the consuming, irrational love that made her need Justin as she needed air.

She wrenched away from his grasp and turned her back on him. "It isn't mumbo jumbo," she retorted.

"Stop it, Serena."

"I can't."

She felt another tightening of those muscles behind her and flinched with the flash of heat.

But he didn't touch her. The spin of his heels could be heard even on the plush carpeting.

"I'm going to pick up some groceries. We haven't anything edible in here except crackers. Get your things unpacked while I'm gone."

She heard the front door slam as he left, and she brought a knuckle to her teeth and bit down hard.

I'm crazy, she told herself, really crazy. . . . I love him so much, but I'm afraid.

She spun around on the carpet and resurveyed the room for a moment of indecision, then sighed and slipped off her heels, allowing her stockinged feet to sink into the comfortable carpet.

I love him, and I haven't a thing against New York, and I know that he can't just walk away and that Sue can run the museum.

She walked across the room to her suitcase and dragged it into the bedroom. She received a start when she set the suitcase on the bed and the bed suddenly started to dip and weave. She frowned and then laughed. It shouldn't have been a surprise to discover that Justin had a waterbed.

She lay down, wondering if she were going to be able to sleep on the constantly mobile bed. Her slightest twitch brought new waves of motion, but it was nice, relaxing.

Serena stretched out her arms and her hands slid beneath the pillows. She frowned again as her fingers clutched an object. Pulling it out, she discovered an object of clothing that definitely didn't belong.

A very elegant, lacy black bra.

She tossed it across the room as if it were contaminated, felt a wave of searing jealousy strike her, and drove her fist into the pillow with a furious "Damn him!"

She was still lying on the bed—not a thing done—when he returned twenty minutes later.

She heard him calling from the doorway but made no move to rise and assist him. She heard him cursing softly as he struggled to set his bags down on the counter, but she didn't really care. She felt strangely empty, as if the entire affair had been absurd. He had brought nothing but trouble into her life (hadn't Miles Grant died swearing he would find revenge?), and now he had dragged her here to flaunt his past affairs before her. Denise was very probably right—*she* was the one who would fit into his life. *Hell!*, she had already been fitting into his life, and she was so little daunted by Serena that she didn't even give a damn that Justin slept with her.

"Serena?" He was standing in the doorway, and he was very definitely aggravated. The green had almost disappeared from his eyes; they appeared almost as dark as mahogany.

"What the hell are you doing?" he demanded. "Didn't you hear me calling you? I almost dropped the bag with the damn eggs."

"I'm not doing anything," she muttered tiredly, "except thinking that we're both insane." He stared at her hard, and she inclined her head toward the corner of the room where the bra had fallen. "It seems," she added sweetly, "that someone else is still living in *our* room."

"Dammit, Serena!" He was across the room before she could even struggle to a sitting position, straddling across her and catching her wrists when she attempted to elude him.

"I have been dead honest with you, Serena, so don't try flinging things in my face."

She met his relentless eyes and knew she was behaving like an adolescent but couldn't control herself. She was so confused; there were just too many things.

She lowered her lashes over her eyes. "Leave me alone, Justin."

She was startled when he released her hands, then realized he did so only to shift his weight slightly to reach for the hem of her dress and slide it up her thighs.

"Justin, stop it!" she protested, finding herself capable of sheer, catty jealousy.

"Why?" he demanded, not stopping in the least as he pulled the summer linen higher, apparently unaware of the pressure of her arms against him as he reached behind her for the zipper.

Serena kept struggling, which was difficult because her arms became bound by the material as he drew it over her head.

"Because," she garbled, her words furious but distorted against the cloth, "you are not making love to me now . . . here . . . on these sheets—"

"Oh, Serena!" His exclamation was harsh and heated as the dress came over her head and he faced her blazing eyes. "I have a woman who comes in twice a week, and she changes linen."

"Then what is *Denise's* lingerie doing in the bed?"

"I don't know," Justin mumbled, reaching once more behind her back to undo her bra strap. "I assume Denise came in and planted it, hoping to get just such an immature reaction out of you."

"Immature!" Serena tried to clutch her own bra against her chest, but it was whisked away from her clenching fingers. And then she was pressed against him, feeling the heat and friction of his chest despite the shirt he still wore. She wound her fingers into his shoulders by the neck, trying to push away.

"Immature," he repeated calmly, refusing to budge a hair as he sent his hands playing down her spine.

It has to be magic, Serena thought, because I'm really ready to strangle him, and his touch is still . . .

"God dammit, Justin," she charged, "how would Miss Marshall manage to do such a thing?"

He laughed against her ear, and the sound was throaty, stimulating despite all her efforts.

"I guess she still has the key."

"Oh, Justin, I don't believe this! Let me go this instant or—"

"Or?" he queried.

"I mean it, Justin."

He released her, and she fell back to the pillow. The bed began to rock crazily, and between that and his weight still straddled over her, she couldn't move.

And then she realized he was no longer angry, but laughing. Tears of indignation filled her eyes, and she fought hard to keep them from spilling over. "Don't you dare laugh at me!" she hissed. "I can just imagine your reaction if my room had been filled with jockey shorts!"

He still laughed, so hard that she could see his stomach muscles tense and ripple. In a second of seething rage she struck out at him, only to find her wrist caught surely in his quick hand and her body pressed against the floating bed as he laid his weight completely on top of her, only his chest raised slightly so that he could see her face. "Oh, sweetheart," he murmured, to her frigid defiance, "I'm not laughing at you. I'm laughing because we finally have a normal problem!" With a quick roll he was sitting beside her, wrenching his shirt over his head.

Serena quickly noted her freedom and attempted to rise. "I'm glad you find normal problems amusing—"

She had made it to a sitting position, but that was it. As his shirt went flying, he caught her around the midriff, and she fell back, unable to obtain balance quickly as the bed started to wave like an ocean.

"Damn you, Justin—"

She tried to sit again, but he caught the hem of her slip, and

161

as he pulled it from her with a laughing jerk, she sprawled backwards again. He pinned her with weight, kicking off his shoes with his feet, then sliding a hand down her bare midriff to wedge beneath the elastic of her pantyhose and roll it down her hip.

"Justin—"

He smiled but didn't cease, aware as she that her breaths were growing shorter with the manipulation of his fingers. He slid a knee between her thighs to graze the nylon from one leg, then swiftly shifted to repeat the gesture on the other, ignoring her panted threats and pleas all the while. She was trembling like a leaf when she lay naked beneath him.

"Justin—this isn't fair—"

"We wouldn't be anywhere if I believed in fair," he murmured, firmly grazing a rough, heat-eliciting palm up along her thigh, hip, and midriff to cup a breast and bring the nipple erect with an expert manipulation by a finger.

"Justin!"

He held her there, leg wedged between her naked thighs, his own desire potent and burning through the fabric of his jeans, his hand firmly and intimately planted upon her breast, his eyes locked with hers. And then he spoke.

"You have every right to be mad, hurt, and jealous, Serena, but I can't erase my own past. You're trying to conclude that we're both crazy, and so I have to prove to you that we're not, unless simply being madly and deeply—and physically as well as mentally—in love is crazy. I know we're both sane, just like I know we're going to have problems. And I also know that we can solve those problems. Problem number one: we'll have the locks changed tomorrow morning. And we'll buy all new sheets and a damned new bed if you want. Now have you got anything else to bitch about?"

Serena stared into the face above hers, the eyes that were demanding fire, the jawline that was rugged, relentless—and absurdly noble. Beneath her fingers she felt the heated mass of muscle that was beguiling and seductively secure.

"Yes," she snapped, "I certainly do have something to say!"

"What?" he growled.

Her violet eyes softened and half closed provocatively. She raked her fingernails lightly over his back, loving the quivering response, until she slipped her fingers beneath his waistband.

"Could you take your jeans off please?"

She marveled later, curled beside him with her legs still entwined with his, that making love with him was always both so shattering and delicious. He could be unerringly gentle, his light touch driving her wild, then so insatiably demanding that the entire world disappeared into a storm of clouds.

He reached for her, running a finger down her nose, then touching her lips to circle them lazily. She smiled, her eyes still soft and clouded with delicious contentment. "I'm sorry," she whispered, catching his finger with her teeth lightly as she thought of all the arguments she had purposely provoked.

He grinned with his lips in a half curve. "We're going to have to spend a lot of time in bed," he warned her huskily. "You really become a . . . witch . . . when left alone too long!"

Serena flushed and brought her face against the arch of his neck. "Justin, we do have problems to solve."

"We always will."

"Can we really change the locks?"

"First thing in the morning."

"She came to see me, you know."

He wound his fingers into the loose swirls of hair and pulled her head up so that she faced him again.

"Denise?" he asked incredulously.

"Umm," Serena murmured. "She wanted to warn me that she was—not at all worried that you were in lust. She said you'd never marry me, that a 'witch' wouldn't make a good faculty wife."

"And you listened to her?"

Serena heard the thunder of anger creeping into his voice. She chuckled softly. "No, not really. Maybe just a little. Not too much, I guess, because I had forgotten all about it until now. What with everything happening."

163

Justin frowned, not wanting her to think about the staircase and the damned diary Marc had decided to unearth after all those years.

"I am going to marry you this coming Saturday. And I really couldn't give a damn whether or not you make a 'good faculty wife.' I'm not even sure how I feel about the university anymore. Whether I stay or leave will be a decision we eventually make together, okay?"

Serena nodded and leaned back against him, fears temporarily erased, happiness filling her. She was so drowsy and beautifully content that she started in astonishment when the palm of his hand lit sharply upon her derriere.

"What the—"

" 'What the' eggs are going to rot and the milk sour!" Justin laughed in reply. "The groceries, my love. They're still on the counter."

Serena laughed and rose. Justin sprang up behind her and ducked into a closet to produce a robe for himself and a short-sleeved shirt for Serena that covered her to the knees. He started out the door and then paused.

"Go ahead," he told her. "I want to call Jenny and tell her we decided on Saturday and make sure she got a flight."

Serena nodded, then hesitated herself. She walked over to the corner of the room as Justin sat on the bed and pulled an extension phone from a crevice in the headboard.

"What are you doing?" he queried.

Serena picked up the black bra with the tip of her forefinger and thumb and held it away from her body. She smiled sweetly in reply. "I'm disposing of Miss Marshall's property where it belongs," she purred. "In the garbage."

Justin laughed, and Serena proceeded to do just that before digging into the groceries.

They stayed in New York until Wednesday morning. The two days were a very special time of discovery. Serena's fears faded into the background of her mind as she found out more about Justin, and she loved him more with each new discovery. In his way he was a lot like Bill Loren, a man secure enough with himself to grant her both respect and trust. He was fair, assigning a number of household tasks to himself. But he also never pretended that he expected nothing from her, and she knew that theirs would be a near equal marriage. Although he would very often give of himself in deference to her, he wanted a *wife*. She could almost see the years ahead: he would take out the garbage, but for the most part, she would cook. And he would always make sure their cars were in working order, while she would be chief bed-maker. He liked a neat, orderly home.

They spent the majority of their time in the apartment, and both nights she had to hold back a laugh as she watched him while she finished up in the kitchen. He was such a contrast! A massive hulk of sinew sitting in front of the glass doors as the twilight fell over Manhattan, his reading glasses falling down his nose as he frowned in study of a book. He taught her some of the basics of weight lifting, but when he tried to point out certain muscles, they both started laughing and the weights were forgotten. They went jogging in Central Park, except Serena could only make the first half mile, and he wound up carrying her back, to the laughter and applause of many a bystander in the park.

Serena learned that he loved his daughter and was even on good terms with his ex-wife. "Jill was the reason I didn't think I'd ever marry again," he told her. "She cheated like crazy. Except I see now that I didn't give her much of a life. I was dead serious about getting through school. We never went anywhere, and then there was Jenny."

As Justin had promised, the locks were changed.

They spent long hours in the whirlpool, and Serena also talked about herself, telling him about escapades she had gotten into with her brother, and about growing up in a historic city where it was assumed everyone knew that witches had and did practice their craft.

"But you never became a witch?" Justin murmured.

"I never believed in the practices," Serena said.

And Justin became very serious. "The whole secret is in the

words you just said, Serena. I have seen people actually die under voodoo spells. Not because any curse existed, but because the poor victim believed that it did. The mind can be a very powerful weapon. Probably the most powerful on earth. Do you understand me?"

"Yes," Serena whispered. But did she? In the Manhattan apartment, when all was secure in his arms, she could tell herself that she did. There were only a few shaky moments when she stood alone that she thought that things were just too beautiful.

Shades of the past. An instant, inexplicable love.

Their first stop when they reached Salem was the courthouse, where they applied for their wedding license.

And although Serena had felt her skin begin to prickle on the return drive to the Golden Hawk, their actual arrival was wonderful. It was just dusk, and Serena discovered that Tom had stayed and that he and Martha had thrown together an engagement party. Susan and a number of her coven were in attendance, as well as a number of the distinguished gentlemen and ladies who made up the chamber of commerce.

The secret staircase wells were secret no more. Tom had had all of the lever-door paneling removed and her bedroom door repaired.

And most conspicuous of all, the portrait of Eleanora was forever gone. Even Marc made an appearance to tell her he and Tom had donated both the picture and the diary to the historical society.

Serena would have kissed Marc, except that she still felt terribly awkward. He and Justin had greeted one another cordially enough, and Serena discovered with an inner amusement that Marc had asked Justin how he felt about his old room being taken over by a ghost-writer.

Justin had agreed, telling Marc, to Serena's surprise, that they wouldn't be around for another two weeks of the summer anyway. They'd be heading somewhere for a honeymoon.

Mildred Donnesy pleaded to keep her new job for the remainder of the summer. Sue told Serena that the museum had been running just fine; her senior citizen assistants had done so well that she had even taken two afternoons off.

"Mildred makes a wonderful witch," Mr. Donnesy claimed glibly, drawing a sharp glance from his wife only to smile guilelessly in return.

In her room when the party had ended, Serena had to admit that it seemed everything was going to be fine. Even the blank portion of her wall—the stairwell was cut off only by a semiattractive wood-carved safety fence—seemed to offer nothing malicious.

Justin came up behind her and slipped his arms around her waist. "How are we doing, witch-lady?" he murmured.

She circled around into his arms and smiled. "Fine, Dr. O'Neill," she said, "just fine."

And she was fine. That night.

Serena went in to work on Thursday morning and enjoyed watching the Donnesys and Bakers so much that she wondered why she had never offered them a chance to work before.

Mildred did make a marvelous witch.

"It's a pity they can't stay on," Sue commented as both she and Serena sat out most of the day in the office, talking.

Serena shrugged. "Both Giles and Pierce have chronic bronchitis. They both have to head south after the summer. The New England winters would literally kill them." She frowned worriedly. "We'll find someone suitable to be your assistant, I'm sure."

Sue laughed. "Honey, finding someone isn't going to be difficult. Half the people I know want the job. The problem at the moment is to decide upon whom I want to bestow the honor! And then the real problem is that—well, I'm sure as hell going to miss you."

Serena smiled. "I'll miss you, too, Sue. But we'll be less than five hours away, probably here every other weekend." She took a sip of coffee and then asked quietly, "Sue, do you think this is insane? I mean getting married so quickly?"

"Not when you're that sure about love," Sue replied. "You need time when you don't know, honey, not when you do. And besides, I went out and spent a fortune on a new dress to stand up for you! Back out on me now, and I'll have to get married Saturday night."

Serena laughed. "Well, if I promise I won't back out, will you help me with another problem?"

"What's that?"

"Help me figure out what I'm going to do with people. Justin wants to have two colleagues and his daughter come up. Okay, listen good and hang with me. The inn has six rooms. Mine, Tom's, and Martha's, and the three we let out. Tom is staying for the weekend, so his room is taken. Justin and I will be leaving Saturday night, which empties my room. Marc has taken Justin's old room, but he'll just have to go home for Friday and Saturday night. The Donnesys and the Bakers will still be in their rooms. Are you still with me? That leaves me with three people and only two rooms—short of space."

"Easy," Sue said. "Justin's professor friends can have the two rooms, and his daughter can stay with me."

"Oh, Sue, I hate to do that to you—"

"Don't be ridiculous. I'm dying of curiosity!"

"So am I," Serena admitted. She shook her head. "I still don't think I believe all this, Sue. Instant husband—and instant sixteen-year-old. And instant New York City—"

"You're starting to sound jittery," Sue warned. "I think you should get out of here and go buy a dress—and a pack of lacy lingerie and anything else you can think of! There's only tomorrow, and then there's Saturday—and then two P.M.!"

"I guess I will go pick up some things," Serena murmured. She glanced at Sue with a frown. "I think it's been a little insulting to realize how dispensable I am!"

"Not to Justin," Sue said softly. "And to be indispensable to a man you love . . . well, that's what counts, honey."

"Thanks, Sue," Serena replied. She collected a few things she had strewn on the desk and dug her purse out from beneath her desk. She smiled as she walked toward the door and then paused.

"Sue, I'm sure Tom has told you about the stairwell and the diary. And that I came out of the stairwell shrieking that Justin . . . was Miles."

Sue glanced at her nails. "Yeah, I heard."

"Well?"

"You were locked in a dark stairwell for hours. It's easy to believe anything in that kind of circumstance."

"Sue!" Serena persisted. "No vibes at all?"

"I've liked Justin from the beginning, Serena, and I always told you so."

Serena smiled with worried eyes and left. I am fine, she told herself. I know I was being silly. I know a dark stairwell can make you think anything.

Then why was Sue hedging?

She wasn't hedging; if she didn't believe things would be okay, she would say something, she would try to stop me.

And oh, brother! What is happening to me! I don't believe in any of this, and I tease Susan constantly about her "vibes."

Disgusted with herself, she forced her mind to concentrate on the excitement and wonder of getting married, committing herself to Justin for life and receiving the commitment in return. She went into her favorite boutique and almost immediately found what she wanted—*the* special dress, a pale mauve that hugged her figure and actually made her eyes look violet to herself. The wedding would be small, just those who had attended the party and Justin's friends and his daughter. And it would take place at the inn.

But although she wouldn't be a young bride in frothy white again, it would be even more of an occasion to her because there were still times that she had to shake her head with a certain awe at the fact that Justin was really hers . . . forever.

He greeted her at the door when she came home. "Jenny gets into Boston tomorrow night at five. Flight 307 from Cincinnati. Coming with me to pick her up?"

Serena nodded happily and kissed him. "Of course. Oh, Justin, I hope she likes me!"

He kissed her nose. "She's going to love you."

It was a nice night. They spent the evening talking with Tom, and Serena was thrilled to see how well the man she adored and the brother she loved dearly got along. It was very late when she fell asleep in Justin's arms, and her dreams should have been sweet.

They were terrifying.

She was awakened from them by a piercing scream of horror that filled the night air with jagged, hysterical shrieks.

And she was the one screaming.

CHAPTER TEN

A hand clamped firmly over her mouth.

"Dammit to hell, Serena! Shush! You're going to have the whole house up here thinking I'm beating you to death!"

Justin spoke with a thin veil of soothing humor over an irritation he simply couldn't bury. He released her mouth slowly, whispering, "What the hell is the matter with you?"

Serena sprang from the bed, shaking. She stared at him in the moonlit dimness of the room, her eyes wide with an unfathomable fear. She tried to speak, failed, and finally managed, "Justin—it can't be. It simply can't be. Something terrible is going to happen."

To his amazement she spun from him and headed for the door. He leapt after her, reaching the door before her and catching her in his arms as he blocked the exit from her.

"You're damned right something terrible is going to happen," he charged her. "You'll get to see a real jealous fit, and I will start beating you if you go running out of this room stark naked."

She paused and blinked, and he realized she had only now become fully conscious. He shook her slightly, whispering a sharp "Serena!" She stared into his eyes, lips trembling, then

171

threw herself into his arms. She was still shaking with sobs of terror.

He let her cry for a second, smoothing back her hair as she drenched his chest with tears. Then he picked her up and walked her back to the bed where he laid her down and pulled the covers around her before joining her, propped up on an elbow as he held her securely.

"It can't be, Justin," she murmured, her eyes meeting his clearly but still liquid with tears.

"Serena, you had a dream," he told her firmly. "And I'm not throwing my life away because of a dream."

"But—"

"Tell me about it."

"I . . ." She wanted to tell him, to explain, but she knew her explanation would be weak because description couldn't make him understand the overwhelming terror she had felt.

"Tell me, Serena," he insisted softly, hand firm and securely steadying over her hip as he lay beside her, touching her with the warm length of his body.

"You were coming at me, Justin, but all I could really see were your eyes. And the deeper I looked, the more I could see that the brown within them was actually yellow fire. You had no pupils, Justin. . . . Your eyes were actually fire. . . ."

She paused, biting a lip as she realized he had to think she was crazy to scream like a child over a dream about fire in his eyes.

"Go on," he urged her softly.

"You were calling to me, and I couldn't tell what you were saying. I felt that I had to go to you, and yet that if I did I would catch fire. . . . I . . . I just couldn't tell if you were trying to help me . . . or . . . or burn me with the flame. And then . . ."

"Then what?"

"You kept getting closer, and I was paralyzed with fear. And then suddenly the fire wasn't in your eyes at all. It burst between us and the flames reached into the sky and they were blue with intensity. . . ."

"And then you woke up," he concluded softly.

"Yes."

He hugged her close to him, soothing her with gentle strokes over her shoulder and arm. "Serena, I would never hurt you."

"I believe that, Justin," she murmured, "I mean, not intentionally. But, Justin, I'm so frightened! It's just like the dream. I want you so badly, but I can't tell what's wrong. . . ."

"There's nothing wrong," he said firmly, "and I'm not going to allow anything to be wrong. Half your problem is this damn house—and we'll be out of it on Sunday."

"Justin, it isn't the house. Neither of us believes in haunted houses. I've lived here all my life, and I never had a problem until you . . . until we—"

"Serena," he interrupted firmly. "You're right—I don't believe in haunted houses. And I'm sure you don't either. But I do believe in the power of suggestion. You have all this Eleanora nonsense on your mind, and it's giving you nightmares. I'm telling you right now, Serena—I love you. And I don't give a damn about what happened to Eleanora Hawk centuries ago. We're going to be married on Saturday if I have to drug you and drag you down the aisle—because I know you love me too."

"No, Justin, our lives—"

"Serena," he whispered softly, "it was a dream, and yes, dreams can be very terrifying! But I'm here, and I'm going to hold you through the night, and I won't even try to sleep until—"

"Oh, don't you understand, Justin? It isn't only me! When that fire came up, I didn't know who was going to suffer . . . to pay—me, or *you!*"

"Serena," he said, laughing. "Look at me, sweetheart. What do you think is going to happen to me?"

"Justin—"

"I'll always be very careful—"

"Dammit. Don't patronize me, Justin!"

Serena felt his muscles tense, saw the telltale tic in his jaw. "And don't push the limits of my patience!" he exclaimed in return, his whisper harsh. "Now it's the middle of the night. Let's get some sleep."

"I can't sleep, I keep remembering—"

"Well," he murmured, and a subtle difference came to his tone. "I'll bet I can make you forget all about it. If I'm going to be awake anyway . . ."

Tom Hawk had been dreaming himself when his eyes suddenly flew open. He was glad to be awakened; his own dream wasn't pleasant, but whether he had actually heard or sensed his sister's scream, he didn't know.

He bolted from his bed and secured a terry robe around himself before flinging open his door and racing down the hallway.

In front of Serena's door he paused in consternation, his hand halted in the middle of intent before he could tap on the new wood.

The room was quiet. He couldn't go flying into her room when she was sleeping with her fiancé. If he had imagined the scream, they would both think him insane.

And if he weren't careful, O'Neill would start thinking the whole family was bats.

But what if O'Neill wasn't entirely what he seemed. What if Serena had screamed. What if the muscle-bound Ph.D. was a little off the wall himself, threatening Serena to silence while he performed sick deeds.

Hell, Tom Hawk, he told himself beneath his breath as a smile at his own absurdity curled his lips, you are half-bats.

He glanced at the door again. Not a sound was coming from it. But he had been worried about his sister, and when he worried, he was usually right to do so.

With his face twisted in a mask of uncertainty, he leaned his ear against the door and began to hear murmuring.

And then his sister's voice. Soft . . . almost a purr.

"Oh . . . Justin . . ."

Tom drew his ear from the door as his face turned pink. Sheepishly he made his way back to his own room.

In the morning the Golden Hawk itself seemed to sleep late. No one appeared for breakfast at eight, which was fine because Martha was still sleeping herself. Mildred Donnesy was the first to awaken, and then she woke up her poor husband with a swat, reminding him that they were among the employed and that the museum had to open. They and the Bakers departed quietly.

Serena awoke at eleven to see Justin zip up a pair of beige trousers and pull a navy knit shirt over his head. His hair was wet, and she realized a bit resentfully that he had already jogged and showered and was on his way out.

His eyes fell upon her as he clipped on his watch and collected his keys. He arched a brow. "Good morning."

"Good morning," she mumbled in return, curling her arms around her pillow.

"You okay?"

Serena nodded slowly. He had managed to make her forget the dream. And now, in daylight, it did seem a little foolish.

He walked over to the bed and smiled as he leaned down to kiss her. She was always a vision to him. Her chestnut hair was billowed in wild disarray about her, her violet eyes appeared sweetly sensuous in their drowsy state.

He touched her lips swiftly, then backed away. "I'm getting out of here quickly," he laughed, knowing she was still a little too out-of-it to understand why. "I have to pick up my suit, and I want to stop by AAA to pick up a few maps. And Martha asked me to stop by the florist and make sure they have the delivery set for early in the morning." He waited a minute, wondering if she would protest.

She didn't. She smiled vaguely and closed her eyes again.

"Don't forget, we have to pick up Jenny at five."

"I won't forget," Serena mumbled.

The click of the door when he left snapped Serena out of her drowsiness. She stretched for a minute, glanced at the clock on the nightstand, and groaned. Damn, it was late.

She bathed quickly and decided to wear a skirt and a tailored blouse with an edge of ruffling down the front. The outfit, in shades of summer mauve, was neither too businesslike nor

175

fussy. Perfect for meeting Justin's daughter, and since they would have to leave for Logan Airport with a good hour to spare on a Friday night, she didn't think she'd have a chance to change again.

She was surprised to find her brother in the kitchen popping bread into the toaster, his usually bright expression definitely dour. She raised a brow at him as she checked the coffeepot.

"Rotten night," he murmured.

"Must be an epidemic," Serena replied lightly, grateful to see that there was coffee in the pot. "Where's Martha?"

"She went into town to collect a few supplies for tomorrow. Most of the food is going to be delivered, and the florists are supposed to do the arrangements in the house, but you know Martha. She wants everything perfect."

Serena smiled. "My wedding," she said, laughing, "and I've barely done a thing."

"That's allowed," Tom said, grinning, "since it's almost a shotgun affair. Want some toast?"

"Thanks."

"Good. I'll make your toast if you'll pour my coffee."

"I didn't get the bad end of the stick in that deal," Serena agreed.

A few minutes later they sat across from each other at the table. Tom looked at his sister quizzically, and she half smiled and half frowned as she caught his stare. "What?" she asked.

"How come you had a bad night?" he said.

"Oh . . . a dream."

Tom swallowed a bite of toast and rinsed it down with a sip of coffee. "I thought I heard you scream," he said. He started to blush. "In fact, I came racing out of my room to your door . . . but . . . well, you weren't screaming anymore. And I . . . well, I knew you were all right. I mean, not in any pain."

Serena started flushing too, and then both brother and sister broke into laughter, still flushing. "I'm sorry I woke you," Serena murmured, trying to change the subject.

"Oh, I was glad you woke me. I was having a horrendous dream myself."

176

"You were?" Serena felt her body tense in some type of strange anticipation. "About what?"

Tom shrugged and smiled gently in reply to the anxiety in his sister's eyes. "Not about you, or Justin, or anything relevant. Just strange. And . . . painful."

"Tell me about it," Serena demanded.

"I'd rather not. It would just bring up a lot of long-ago pain for you to dwell on too."

"I don't understand."

"I was dreaming about Mom."

"Mom," Serena repeated, bewildered. Then she said softly, "Tom, you should tell me about the dream. Justin made me tell him about mine, and it made me feel better. And, Tom, it's always going to hurt us both a little about our parents, but they've been gone ten years. We can both talk about it now."

Tom shrugged again, then grimaced. "It was really kind of crazy. I felt like I knew Mom was in the house, and I could hear the plane. But I couldn't get to her. All I could do was hear the plane. That funny soaring noise. And then there was an explosion, and flames leaping high and—hey, Serena, what's the matter?"

She had jumped to her feet and gone as white as chalk. "Serena, it was all long ago. Damn, I knew I shouldn't have said anything—"

"That's it!" Serena shrieked, "A fire—a plane! Oh, Jesus, Tom, that's it. Justin was right; he's strong, so little can hurt him, he's like the Rock of Gibraltar, but one thing could kill him, and that's his daughter, he loves her so much—"

"Serena." Tom jumped beside her in alarm. "What are you talking about? Calm down—"

"I can't. I have to find Justin. I have to make him get Jenny off that plane—"

Shaking off her brother's touch, she was outside and into her car before he could stop her. He was just in time to be covered by the dust as the wheels sent it flying.

177

Justin had already left the cleaners. She didn't catch up with him until he was leaving the AAA office, and then she was so incoherent it was minutes before he could understand a thing she was saying.

He was patient at first when he tried to calm her, but his patience fled fast to become irritation. He sternly forced her to quiet down and speak slowly, then ducked her inside to the far corner of a dimly lit lounge, ordering them both stiff drinks.

He wouldn't let her speak again until she had taken several sips.

Then she tried to get ahold of herself and plead as rationally as she could.

"Justin, please, we're wasting time. You have to stop Jenny from getting on that plane. Don't you see, it's your turn—"

"Serena! I've gone about as far with all this as I can go. It is not my turn for anything! And I'm not going to have my daughter miss the wedding because you have nightmares."

Serena knew the set to his face, the iron lock to his strong jaw. She stared at him helplessly, then fell silent and quietly finished her drink, feeling the heat and intensity of his eyes all the while.

She stood up and gazed down at him, defeated. "There won't be a wedding tomorrow, Justin. I can't marry you."

He caught her wrist. "You are going to marry me tomorrow."

He didn't like her reply. She didn't try to fight him. She merely lifted her eyes sadly to his. "I doubt if you'll want to marry me anymore tomorrow," she said quietly.

And with a dignified little hike to her shoulders, she left him.

He stared after her for a long while.

Serena didn't go into the house when she drove home; she left her car and started walking blindly, and her walk brought her to the pond. She sat down upon the damp earth, not caring that dirt and soft, sandy mud covered her skirt and stockings.

It was strange, but at the pond she didn't feel anything. The terrible feeling of something terrible about to happen left her. It was almost as if a veil of tranquility had fallen over her.

She didn't know how long she sat. But sometimes she would glance up at the sun and see that it was moving across the sky. Twilight was coming.

And twilight made tears slip silently down her cheeks even as a smile of memory tugged at her lips.

She could remember that first time so clearly.

He had risen from the water, and as soon as she had quit choking, she had looked at him and known that no matter what the consequences, she wanted him, desperately, more than she had ever wanted anything in her life.

And that very first time, as total strangers, their lovemaking had been beautiful. He had known just where and when to touch her; she had known his incredible physique in return.

And despite all the lies she had told herself, she must have known even then she loved him, because once he had touched, she had known that she had always craved his touch.

"Oh, Justin," she whispered fervently aloud, "I love you so much. I would fight anything to be with you, but I love you too much to take a chance on hurting you."

The trees whispered in a soft breeze, and the water of the pond rippled, brushed to little peaks of shimmering sparkles as it caught and reflected the last sun of the day.

She didn't feel him behind her. She had no awareness at all until he spoke, and then her back seemed to stiffen and freeze.

"There was a problem with Flight 307 from Cincinnati," he said, and she was stunned to realize that his voice was merely calm and authoritative, nothing more. "A small fire broke out in flight, but the plane landed safely. Several passengers were hospitalized, but all are reported in stable condition."

Serena kept staring at the pond. She wanted to talk, but she couldn't. She wanted to scream at him, to beg that he go away, to tell him that he tortured both of them.

He sat down beside her and drew her chin around gently with his thumb and forefinger.

"Serena—Jenny wasn't on the flight."

Her eyes widened as she stared at him, and she started to tremble uncontrollably. He slipped an arm around her and brought her head to rest against his shoulder.

"I called her, sweetheart, just as you asked. Everything is all right."

Serena started to cry again, she couldn't help herself. Silent tears raced down her cheeks. "But, Justin, it isn't! Don't you see—"

"I only see that I love you," he interrupted, "and that you love me. And that I want you to be my wife."

"Justin, I can't . . ." The words came out in anguish. She was staring at his hand, at the long fingers, at the broad back, and she was thinking that she loved everything about him, from the way his fingers dangled to the way his eyes darkened in passion and even in anger.

"Just suppose," he interrupted her again, "that any of this made sense. Say—hypothetically—that Eleanora and Miles have in some way come back. And now think, Serena, pay close attention to what I'm saying. Eleanora died in that staircase— Miles was able to do nothing. But, Serena, I was able to bring you out. And then we'll take poor Miles. Bereft of the woman he loved, he sickened and died. Say that I was threatened by something happening to someone I loved dearly, my own blood. Jennifer. Nothing happened to her, Serena, because of you. Now suppose, just suppose, hypothetically, that we are talking about shades of the past. Eleanora and Miles loved each other. Their most fervent wishes were to be together. If they have come back, Serena, don't you think they want us to be together, more than anything in the world? That very special love, that recognition of the perfect mate for life? Those were what we all shared, Serena. If anything has come from the past, Serena, it is a cleansing. We can have each other, we can have the beauty and the love they were denied."

Serena listened to Justin, her whole body tense with longing. God, how she wanted to believe him.

She lifted her head from his shoulder and stared at him, her violet gaze demanding all. "You don't believe a word of that, do you, Justin?"

He smiled at her softly. "No. I do not believe in reincarnation, ghosts, spooks, haunts, or spirits."

"But, Justin, I did know about the plane. And Tom and I have often known when one or the other of us was in trouble."

He continued smiling at her, slipping his fingers through her hair and drawing her face close to his. "I don't deny that, Serena. There are many mind bonds that we know little about yet."

Serena didn't know what it was, Justin's supreme confidence and unfaltering love, or the idea that perhaps his story held a note of truth—that maybe they were being saved by the remnants of the past rather than threatened, but suddenly she began to feel a tiny ripple of hope filtering through her body.

"Justin," she murmured, feeling she was drowning a little in the depths of his eyes. "Aren't you worried a little? Just a little? You never know when I'm going to pop up with something like this morning. An insight. Won't you feel a bit like you're married to a freak?"

"I always did think I was getting a bit of a *witch*," he replied, and his comment was both dry and affectionate. "No, Serena, you don't scare me. What you and Tom have is wonderful. And as long as you don't start reading palms, I'll keep you nice and sane by always following any really strong hunch you have. Except that I don't think it will be that often. I do strongly believe in the power of suggestion—as you know—and a lot has been happening around here lately." He drew her even closer, and he kissed her, his love, his need, and his passion clearly portrayed in a possession both fierce and tender. Thought slipped away as he held her, his tongue claiming hers, his lips and teeth bruising in their ardency. He held her head with one hand and crushed her torso against his with the other. He robbed her of strength, and then it seemed that he returned it tenfold.

Finally he pulled away. Clutching her head between splayed fingers, he stared into her eyes. "Don't deny me, sweet witch.

Please! What happened to the beautiful level woman of logic? You can't really believe that a poor murdered girl would come back to wish us harm! You can't believe that, Serena; I don't believe that you believe it!"

"I . . ."

He was right, and she wanted to answer him, but she couldn't.

His eyes darkened, and the tight, controlled fierceness of his tone continued, and he as suddenly released her and stood.

"I love you, Serena. I want you to be my wife. Everyone has problems—and most people have a few odd quirks. Now and then, yours might be a little odder than most. I don't care. Now I have been sitting in a pile of mud for half an hour trying to talk some sense into you. I am offering you a lifetime of love that can and will combat any obstacle we come across—if we just let it. I want to work toward all the usual things. A good marriage, a nice home, maybe a dog, or maybe a cat, and two point five children—or whatever it is. I'm going to take off my very muddy clothes and jump into that pond. And you're going to decide if you love me enough to live *our* lives together. And I'm warning you right now that if you do jump in the pond, you will never attempt to tell me again that you're not going to marry me and spend your life with me. I'll show you just what good weight lifting can do for arm strength when I turn your bewitching little rear-side red enough to last a hundred lifetimes. Got it?"

He had half torn his clothing in a vehement effort to remove it. The last words were huffed out as he hopped to remove his shoes and socks.

He stood there naked and glared at her menacingly after his final words—then jumped into the pond.

Serena stared after him, incredulous at first that he would speak to her so, then angry. Then she suddenly found herself laughing because she was angry.

And then she stood up and slipped out of her clothing as she watched him swim away without a backward glance.

Because if there were a haunting of days gone past, that haunting was of love. Undeniable, beautiful, wonderful—love.

She plunged into the water after him and swam as quickly as she could, huffing and puffing for breath as she reached him. He stopped and watched her warily with a lifted brow as he tread water.

"I mean it, Serena," he warned, "Come to me now and it's for a lifetime. I do believe in carrying out threats."

She laughed. "I believe you." Her violet eyes shimmered with reflections from the water. "And I am so pleased that you decided to believe in marriage. And wherever we are, I want a nice home too. And a good marriage. And a cat first—witches are supposed to have familiars, you know. Now as to the two point five children—I really insist that we have two, or go all the way to three. The point five bit makes me a little nervous!"

He laughed and drew her into his arms, and together they swam until they could stand in the water. He kissed her again, and she felt all his hunger, all his need, all his love in that kiss. It was the same as it had been that first time, simply, beautifully right. She knew him, she knew that he would demand everything and that he would cherish her in return. For all time. . . .

She pressed closer to him, loving the powerful feeling of the body she knew so well against hers. The sensations were now familiar but forever erotic and wildly provocative. He trailed his hands over her naked form, and she shivered against him, anticipating.

But he suddenly chuckled and held her away. "Sweetheart," he murmured, hazel eyes like the sun in their laughter, "you are one devilishly enticing wicked little witch, but we have to get back."

Serena raised a brow in surprise.

"I want you to meet Jenny."

"Jenny?"

"Yes, I had her change flights. She came in at six by a different airline."

"Oh!" Color suddenly flooded Serena's face. "Oh, Justin, our clothes are all muddy! I can't meet your daughter—"

He caught her beneath the breast as he had the first day and towed her back across the pond, picking her up when he neared the shore to set her down by her clothing.

"We'll sneak up the unhidden staircase and change." He laughed.

"Why didn't you tell me she was here?" Serena demanded as she stumbled back into her clothing.

"I had to have a guarantee there was going to be a wedding first," he replied dryly, stuffing his shirt into his pants. He grabbed her arms while she was still fumbling with her shoes. "Come on."

Serena laughed and followed him, her wet hair flying about her face. She suddenly stopped him before they could break out of the shelter of the trees. "Justin, do you suppose we could get the picture of Eleanora back from the historical society for tomorrow?"

"What?" Serena loved the wary frown that tightened his brow, the strong, relentless command that made his jaw appear like steel.

"Humor me, my love, will you?" Her eyes were bright and dazzling with a conniving plea. "I'd like to have the portrait in the parlor when we're married. I . . . I think it only fair that Eleanora get to be there when we legally become man and wife."

He continued to stare at her for a second, then his frown slowly became a twisted grin.

"Okay, I suppose I can humor you. After all, you have convinced me that one form of the occult does exist."

"I have?" Serena murmured incredulously. "What form of the occult is that?"

He caught her hand and brought it to his lips and brushed her fingers with a kiss as he locked his eyes with hers.

"Magic," he said very softly. "*This* is magic. I believe in magic."

EPILOGUE

It was dusk. Spectral vision time. And as always, she was a vision, the magic of dusk, of dreams. As he opened his eyes, she was simply there, across the expanse of clear water glittering beneath the fading light of day.

She wore a cloak, a black cloak. Her eyes lifted, and she gazed upon the water.

And then she lifted thick lashes and her stunning violet stare fell upon him.

And she smiled, her lips curving full and sensually, as she held all of the secrets of twilight and of dreams.

He returned her smile, his own eyes half closing lazily with expectant delight. Outside, it was snowing. Beyond the glass enclosure of the misting pool, the weather was raw; blankets of white fell about them, misting all within the glass to combine with twilight and become . . .

Magic.

Her eyes lowered again; her secret smile became deeper. Then she spun about, a wealth of chestnut floating about her like a gold-tinged mantle. And as she circled she raised her arms, the black cape opened, and he saw that beneath it she was beautifully and splendidly . . . naked.

Her eyes touched upon his again, and in them he read the

love that was such an integral part of both of them. So many things were said with that look. And he answered them all. His return smile and the brow he arched high were indicative also of a love they no longer questioned but accepted as a special gift . . . from time, from God.

She knew that after five years of marriage he appreciated the ritual. And yet his eyes challenged her with amusement and query. There were things to consider this time. . . .

But she knew that if a hearty soul should pass the glass facing the sand in the snow nothing could be seen within the enclosure.

Dusk and mist now served as a privacy shield where once the forest had been their enclosure.

And she knew, too, that they would not be disturbed from within. Tom had taken Sue and Jenny and the new baby to dinner, very carefully braving the snow to give them this time.

Dusk and twilight magic.

She felt a little thrill of laughter build within her; the stare he gave her was calm and cool . . . almost insolent with confidence. And yet he had to be puzzled.

She was very aware of him as she stretched high and allowed the cape to drift to the floor.

And that sultry awareness had a devastating effect. He felt everything within him tighten, burn and pulse as he watched her.

She was neither slim nor heavy, but some plane of perfection in between. Her high, very full breasts were tipped with deep rouge, proud and inviting. They lusciously curved above a long, slender ribcage that tapered neatly to a minuscule waistline, the ivory skin like satin as it dipped in twilight shadow to the hollow of her belly.

She had changed so little.

And his reactions to her had changed even less. There was something still softly innocent about her, even as she wantonly seduced him. And it was that special touch of innocence which combined with the instinctive sensuality that staggered him with a shaft of raw, shattering desire. Yet even that desire was touched by magic; it was a very male need to conquer and to dominate with selfish possession, but it was tempered by a need to cherish with a tenderness every bit as intense but which had grown in the five years of their marriage.

She raised a brow in return to his. For a second in time—or was it an eternity?—she stretched higher, the gleaming ivory of her body glistening in the soft light, and then she disappeared into the water, making its crystal surface ripple in tiny waves.

He stared at the water, then glanced at the glass enclosure. That little witch, he thought, and then he laughed with the realization that the mist shielded them.

And then he wasn't laughing, but the heated roar of his blood suddenly became almost painful. Damn, did he need her, and it had been so long, and the invitation was so sweetly, poignantly clear.

He stripped off his swimming trunks, then dove into the water and caught her beneath the surface, slipping his arms around her as they kicked up together. He gave her a second for a single breath, then kissed her, a sizzling heat in the hungry touch of lips and tongue. He released her with a little objection, kicked the water with a smooth scissors kick, and brought them both to the edge of the pool.

"I'm not sure whether to throttle you straightaway or love you to death," he murmured, his tone half threat and half groan.

"Love me," she whispered, her eyes dazzling with the reflection of the water. "We're completely alone." With her words she began to plant devilish little kisses along his shoulders. He felt as if lightning sizzled his body.

"Your brother . . . Sue . . ." he stated, his words beginning to trail in spite of his best efforts. "My daughter . . . our son . . ."

"All gone. For at least three hours."

He took her lips again, then his mouth brushed a delightful pattern along her throat and dipped beneath the water to nuzzle her breasts. She gasped with the pleasure, slipping her slender legs around him to stay above surface. He released his hold upon the tile, and they both careened downward, but his assault continued, and he slid his hands low over her spine and to her buttocks as he ran his kisses lower and lower.

Another kick brought them both back up for air, and this time he carried them to the shallow end of Tom's Cape pool.

"Serena," he demanded, eyes dark and stern. "Is it okay now? If you've driven me this crazy and I wind up hurting you . . ."

She closed her eyes and clung to him, almost weeping. "It's time, my love, the exact date the doctor said was okay after the baby, and if you don't take me soon, you will hurt me, I'll be in agony!"

He laughed, and then he wasn't laughing because desire very definitely could hurt. But though his blood pounded within his head and raced like fire through his system, he held himself back, kissing and caressing her within the water, thrilling ever further to her hands and lips upon his body. He intended to set the pace; it would be the first time after a long time, and as he cherished her, he played very carefully upon her body until he felt the moist welcoming heat that assured him she was ready for his ardor.

She cried out his name with delirious happiness, and there, at the water's edge, the magic pulsed between them. Need made it an instant inferno where they merged and flew and drifted quickly . . . but together.

He was smiling, his eyes half-closed with wonderful release, as he caught her eyes. He slipped an arm around her and rolled, bringing them both splattering back into the water. "What?" Serena sputtered, but he had already rested his head upon the tile edge and drawn her against his chest so that they could luxuriate in the weightless drift of the pool. His breath touched her ear as he spoke softly.

"I missed you," he murmured.

"We've never been apart . . ."

"You know what I mean." He bit her ear reproachfully and then murmured, "For a new mother you look marvelous. Aren't you glad I got you started jogging?"

Serena chuckled, caressing his fingers idly as they lay over her midriff. "Actually, you're the one who's lucky you talked me into jogging!"

He pulled his fingers from her touch to run them over her stomach, almost flat now, and the baby was just six weeks old. They smiled together, aware that both thought of the tiny son they both adored, but were still learning to adjust to as parents.

As Justin had always warned her, they did have their problems. But they always worked at solving them. And love was the key.

They were silent for several seconds as the water cooled them, lapping their flesh with the slight waves and ripples. Then Justin suddenly hugged her more tightly to him.

"That was sweet," he murmured. "The black cloak and the water, I mean. You know, I never forget the day we met. I can still close my eyes and see it step by step in detail."

Serena lifted a finger to kiss. "So can I. . . ."

He hesitated a moment, then asked, "Do you ever think about Eleanora and Miles anymore?"

"Yep."

"You do?" His eyes had been closed; he opened them warily and twisted his head to see her face. Her eyes were closed; her lips were curved in a half smile.

She must have sensed his eyes upon her, but she kept her own closed. "I think," she said sweetly, "that they must be resting very peacefully in their graves."

He chuckled softly. "All ghosts put to rest."

Her eyes flicked open, and she started at him impishly. "And all of our human haunts, too! I'm ever so glad Denise found herself that fighter to marry. You see, you thought she loved your position and your money, but it was your muscles all along!"

"Very cute, darling. What about Marc? I think he married your 'witch' replacement faster than she replaced you!"

Serena giggled. "Maybe we should both be a bit insulted. It didn't take either of them long to get over us!"

"That, my darling, is what love is all about. When it's right, it's right, and nothing in the world matters."

"I don't know," Serena contradicted. "Tom and Sue knew each other for years, and it's only been these last six months that they've decided they're madly in love!"

"There are exceptions to every rule," Justin noted with mock indignity. He heard the soft mercury of her laughter in return and then smiled. It might be twilight, but his world was as bright and brilliant as the sun. It was as if that long-ago day at the pond had ended everything, all fears, all terrors. They had been married as planned, down to the picture of Eleanora being set above the fireplace for the ceremony. And since that day Serena had been plagued by neither dreams nor accidents.

Yet if she told him it was going to rain, he always brought his umbrella. It was nice to have a wife one could depend upon with far more accuracy than the weatherman.

And it was nice to see life unfold. He had decided to continue teaching. Serena could make him laugh about the politicking. And she was absolutely charming at his functions, her eyes gleaming like amethysts when they met his in secret, loving laughter.

Summers and weekends throughout the year they spent at the Golden Hawk, keeping the old historical site cared for and preserved, and checking in on the Museum of Fact and Fantasy.

Serena had never been bored; she had picked up her bachelor's degree in psychology and often argued him under the table.

They had their house out on Long Island, their cat—and a dog and a canary—and now they had their wonderful tiny son who kept them both busy.

I have everything, he thought, and he closed his eyes tightly in a moment of sheer gratitude.

He opened his eyes again and pulled his wife tightly against him.

But most of all, I have her.

"How long did you say they would all be gone?" he asked innocently.

She turned in his arms, violet eyes meeting his just as guile-lessly. "At least three hours," she said solemnly.

He lifted her into his arms and carried her up the pool steps. "Then let's go make a little more magic, shall we?"

She raised a cryptic brow with a wicked half smile, and he laughed huskily.

"Oh, I do—I do—I—do—do—believe in magic!"